A Dark Book Club

Also by Alice Zogg

Stand-Alone Mysteries

A Bad Apple
Exposing the Past
No Curtain Call
The Ill-Fated Scientist
Accidental Eyewitness
A Bet Turned Deadly

R. A. Huber Mysteries

Evil at Shore Haven
Guilty or Not
Murder at the Cubbyhole
Revamp Camp
Final Stop Albuquerque
The Fall of Optimum House
The Lonesome Autocrat
Tracking Backward
Turn the Joker Around
Reaching Checkmate

A Dark Book Club

ALICE ZOGG

aventine
press

This book is a work of fiction.

Published by Aventine Press
55 East Emerson St.
Chula Vista CA 91911
www.aventinepress.com

ISBN: 978-1-955162-15-9

Library of Congress Control Number: 2022914276
Library of Congress Cataloging-in-Publication Data
A Dark Book Club/ Alice Zogg
Printed in the United States of America

In memory of Leo, my dear brother

CREDITS

A big thank you to Rita Lossett for allowing me a glimpse into a docent's volunteer work at zoos across the United States. My daughter has moved to a different part of the country, but she did not shy away from the tedious job of proofreading another one of my works. I could not do it without you, Franziska. My appreciation goes to Gayle Bartos-Pool for her great editing skills. She has also moved away from California, yet continues to be my friend and mentor. My husband and I have made some changes in our lives as well. That does not alter the fact that I have Wilfried's quiet but steady support.

CHAPTER 1

On a sunny Monday at the beginning of December, Katherine Scherrer was taking her five-year-old granddaughter, Caitlin, to a county zoo in Southern California. She was impressed with the girl's stamina. They had seen the large elephant exhibit, walked around the east part of the zoo, from the wild cats to the bird aviary, all the way up to view the bears. They had stopped for lunch at one of the eateries, then continued on to the monkey and chimpanzee habitats.

Now they were watching the zebras. Apparently, it was mating season.

"Grandma!" Caitlin exclaimed. "Are they fighting?"

"Uh... they're just playing," Katherine replied.

"One is giving the other a piggyback ride. How fun!"

Suzanne Morlett, volunteering as a docent at the zoo, had finished her tour guide duties for the day and was on her way to the main exit. She heard the little girl's comment and, amused, stopped her stride and lingered for a moment, making eye contact with the child.

Then she did a doubletake and stared at the adult, excited, and called out, "You're Katherine Scherrer, right?"

Katherine nodded.

"What an extraordinary coincidence. The members of our book club voted to read your latest mystery for January, and we'll discuss it the second Wednesday of February."

"I'm flattered."

Suzanne summoned up her courage and asked, "Would you consider joining us for the discussion?"

Katherine's impulse was to decline the invitation, and as she was trying to think of an easy way to refuse without hurting the other's feelings, she was relieved to feel the tug at her arm as her grandchild pleaded, "I need to go to the bathroom."

"We'd better hurry and find one, then," she said to the child. And to the docent, "Happy reading."

"I can see you're in a rush but here's my card. Please give me a call," Suzanne said, handing it over.

On that December evening, full of eagerness, Suzanne told Brian, her husband, all about the encounter.

And she added, "I recognized her right away. She looked exactly like the photo on the back cover of her book. I was surprised, though, how tiny she is. Must be about five foot two inches and probably weighs less than 100 pounds. My guess is she's in her late fifties. The little girl with her was most likely her grandkid. What a stroke of luck to have run into her. I can't wait to tell the rest of the book club members that *the* Katherine Scherrer may join us in February!"

"Don't get carried away," Brian warned. "She may not be interested and might have tossed your business card already."

CHAPTER 2

One morning at the end of January, Katherine was staring at her computer screen. She had a vague plot idea for a new book but could not bring herself to write a single intelligent paragraph. She deleted the text she had typed so far, closed her eyes, and reminisced.

The holidays had come and gone. Although toned down that year with only her close relatives, thanks to the new Covid variant, she had celebrated Christmas with her son and his family. New Year's Eve had found her alone at home, ringing in the new year on TV like she had done ever since Karl, her husband, had passed. It was close to four years now that he had lost his battle with cancer, but she still missed him terribly.

She found refuge in writing. When plotting her stories, she was able to tune the real world out and loose herself in her characters. She was first and foremost a mystery writer but had tried her hand at a couple of thrillers and even a memoir. She chose to pen serious subject matters, but had a knack for adding a bit of lighthearted banter to dialogue in just the right places. For those who knew her well in real life, she was known to have a bit of a warped sense of humor.

Her thoughts switched to what her son and daughter-in-law had pressed her on recently. "Mom, you should sell the house and buy a condominium in a safe and gated community. Your home is too big for just one person, and too remote," she was told. Sure, they would like me to live in Pasadena, preferably right next door to them, she thought. No way is that going to happen. I love them both, and my granddaughter Caitlin is my special sweetheart, but this home here in Lake View Terrace is where I have all my memories of Karl, and where I'm going to stay.

She reminisced further. The kids call the area "remote" but everything - - grocery store, pharmacy, and the nearest mall - - is a short drive away. I have the Angeles Forest Mountains right in my backyard and cherish the hikes we used to take on their trails. I'm not wedged in to neighbors' houses like a can of sardines, but the few neighbors I do have are established residents, having lived here for decades. I know they would give me a helping hand, if needed. When I'm away, they take in my mail and keep an eye on the place. In short, I like the neighborhood and am here for good.

She looked back up at her screen. It's no use; I'm not getting any work done right now. Might as well go for a walk to clear my head. Inspiration may come, she decided.

The temperature was mild, close to 70 degrees, and called for a lightweight jacket. On her way out the door, she grabbed a thin windbreaker out of the coat closet in the hall. She was not in the habit of carrying a purse when going for a neighborhood walk but simply stuffed her phone, ID, and keys into her pockets. When doing so on that day, her fingers touched something already in her right-hand pocket.

She pulled the object out and saw that it was a business card from someone named Suzanne Morlett, who was listed as a librarian. Katherine knew no one by that name and at first wondered how the card got into her jacket. She tried to remember when she'd worn that particular coat last. Then she suddenly recalled the brief encounter with the woman at the zoo. She remembered that she had been in a hurry to find a bathroom and had tucked the card away, not giving another thought to it, nor the woman.

She looked at the card more closely now. So, this woman works at the Montrose Library. Makes sense. She must be a bookworm, since she told me that she was a member of a book club. As Katherine strode along Kurt Street, she mused, my rule has been not to get involved in book clubs and such, but hey, why not? My signing tours have long been cancelled and so are all writers' conferences for the current year. I haven't had a single in-person event in ages. Sure, they are held virtually, but it's just not the same. I don't do well on Zoom and truly miss the interaction with fellow authors, as well as with fans.

Also, these people have bought my book or checked it out of the library. The least I should do is show my appreciation by being present when they discuss it, she thought. Once back at home, she had made up her mind and called the number listed on the business card.

Suzanne picked up on the second ring and gushed, "Oh, Ms. Scherrer, I'm so happy to hear from you. I hope you've decided to join us for the chat of your book?"

"Call me Katherine. And yes, I have. Unless it conflicts with my calendar. I believe you said the meeting was in February?"

"Correct. We meet in the evenings of the second Wednesday of each month. The discussion of your book will be Wednesday, February 9."

"I can do that date and am familiar with the Montrose Library. What time?"

Suzanne corrected, "Oh we don't meet at the library. We used to, but since the pandemic, the book club meetings are at my house at 7:00 p.m. If that's too early for you, I can schedule it for later."

"Where are you located?"

"Also in Montrose."

"7 o'clock is fine. By the way, you're a librarian, so what were you doing that day at the zoo, all by yourself?"

Suzanne giggled and said, "I see your mystery writer instinct at work! To answer your question, I volunteer as a docent at the zoo once a week."

Then she gave her address, which Katherine took down, and the wheels of both their futures were set into motion.

CHAPTER 3

On Wednesday, February 9, Suzanne was loading the dinner dishes into the dishwasher when her sixteen-year-old son, Warren, said, "See you later, Mom," as he headed toward the front door.

"Drive carefully and get home by 10:00!" she shouted, but already heard the door click shut.

Brian came out of the master bedroom and said, "Try not to be an overprotective mom. He's driving to his friend's house, less than three miles away."

"I can't help worrying. He got his license only two weeks ago and is already driving at night."

She had to admit that her husband was right. She'd worried herself sick when their first-born started to drive, and now he was a freshman, away at college, out of their control and doing just fine. Then she concentrated on getting ready for their company.

As Brian helped add the extra leaves to the dining room table - - there would be nine people gathered around it - - he said, "I got the call a moment ago. I need to fly from LAX to Dallas Fort Worth to fill in for a pilot who tested positive with Covid. My bag is packed. After Dallas, I might as well fly directly to JFK for my regular shift."

"Bummer! Do you have to leave right away?"

"I can stay for the meeting but then I'm off."

Fifteen minutes later, the book club meeting was under way. Suzanne had insisted that Katherine sit at the head of the large, rectangular table so that everyone had a clear view of her and vice versa. She had offered coffee, tea, or juice, and then sat down next to the writer.

She started the discussion by addressing the author and saying, "First off, thank you for coming. We are thrilled to have you join us."

With a sparkle in her brown eyes, she went on, "Everyone, please introduce yourselves to our guest, mystery writer Katherine Scherrer. I'll go first, even though we've already met. I'm Suzanne Morlett, librarian at our local library, and as you know, I volunteer as a docent at the zoo every Monday."

Brian took his cue and said, "And I'm her husband, Brian Morlett, a pilot. I'm not an official member, but ever since Suzanne began holding the meetings in our house, I sit in if I'm in town and happen to have read the book in question." He grinned and added, "I've read yours!"

The petite, prim-and-proper lady sitting on his other side, stated, "My name is Violet Richards and I teach at a local high school."

A woman of indeterminable age - - she could be anywhere from 30 to 60, Katherine thought - - dressed in exotic layers of clothing, got to her feet. With a foreign mannerism, she took a bow and said, "The credentials on my driver license are Maxine Dupont, but professionally, I drop the last name and go by Madame Maxine."

As she sat down, Suzanne explained, "Maxine is a psychic."

At the other end of the long table, facing Katherine directly, sat a man who was prematurely balding. "I'm Luke Grey, an accountant. I'm a self-employed financial advisor in Pasadena. And after staring at numbers all day, it is refreshing to read an exciting story and later dissect the book with my fellow book club members," he said.

The young woman to his left simply stated, "My name is Rosalia Acosta. I'm a Spanish interpreter who works in court."

Next to her sat a tall, muscular man who took up almost double the space Rosalia did. "Theo Oxley, here," he bellowed in his baritone. "I'm a police officer and joined the club because my wife begged me to take her place, right before she passed." He chuckled and added, "At first I felt like an elephant among the genteel minded, but I've found my spot within the group."

Last, and immediately to Katherine's right, was an energetic redhead who said, "Charlotte Chadwick. Pleased to meet you. I'm a nurse. Reading relaxes me."

Katherine thought, this is more information than I expected and was willing to get. Let's get on with it already!

Suzanne seemed to have read her mind and stated, "Our meetings start with each person giving the current read either a thumbs-up, thumbs-down, or something in between. Then people elaborate about their vote, giving the reason for it. Let's do that now."

All thumbs were turned to the upright position, except for Charlotte's which leaned from number twelve toward number three on a clock. Interesting, Katherine thought, only one person among this bunch dares to be honest with me present.

People took turns explaining what they enjoyed about the story, which, like most of Katherine's tales, was written in the traditional mystery genre. They were all impressed with the clever plot, mentioned that the clues and red herrings were perfectly placed, thought that the pace was spot-on as far as suspense, and loved the protagonist. In short, the book was a captivating page-turner.

Charlotte was the last person to comment and explained why she did not give it a straight thumbs-up. She said, "Ms. Scherrer, I totally understand that your books are plot driven and this particular mystery was well imagined with a powerful ending, but I would have liked it even better had there been a more detailed description of each character."

Katherine nodded and remarked, "You're not the only one with such an opinion about my tales, but I prefer to leave it to the readers' imagination to picture each character according to their own vision."

After the members had thoroughly discussed the book at hand, they asked some general questions, like, "Where do you get your ideas? Do you outline or write by the seat of your pants? Do you shape your characters after real people you know? How do you decide on location and setting? Katherine had been asked the same questions numerous times at signings, sitting on author panels, or at writer conferences, and she answered all their queries automatically.

Before the evening came to an end, the conversation moved to the Covid pandemic and its newest variant. Violet mentioned that she had had trouble falling asleep at night at the onset of the pandemic in 2020, and that lately, she was suffering from insomnia all over again.

"I have a remedy for that," Katherine shared. "Before going to bed, I soak in the tub for about ten minutes. More often than not, I sip half a glass of wine while doing so. The bath relaxes me and I barely make it under the covers before I drop off to sleep."

While listening as more people voiced their concerns about the virus, the author suddenly chuckled.

Suzanne said, "Care to let us in on the joke?"

"Oh, it's nothing, I'm amused about your priorities, that's all."

"What on earth do you mean?"

"When I arrived at your house you asked me to show proof that I had been fully vaccinated, booster shot and all. It just occurred to me that someone in this group may be more dangerous than Covid."

They all stared at her. Seconds passed without anyone in her audience uttering a word.

Katherine continued, "People can change their hair color and style, change their name, gain or lose weight, move to a different state, or even alter their gender, but I never forget a face, nor a voice."

Suzanne made an attempt at a joke by saying, "I should have insisted that we wear our masks!"

No one laughed. Everyone seemed shaken as Brian asked, "Are you implying that one of us is a criminal?"

Katherine raised her shoulders in a non-committal way and replied, "Maybe."

The pleasant meeting had turned into an event with a sinister undertone. Everyone was suddenly on edge.

Theo Oxley leaned forward, making his chair squeak, and stated, "You're playing a dangerous game, lady!"

Despite Suzanne's seemingly happy chatter as she tried to make light of the situation, the party broke up soon afterwards with everyone eager to leave. Guest and members scrambled out the door at the same time, and Brian grabbed his bag, then kissed his wife good-bye, saying, "I'll be back the 17th or 18th as my schedule looks right now. Love you!"

CHAPTER 4

It took Katherine only 13 minutes to drive from Montrose to her home in Lake View Terrace. At 10 o'clock, she was already soaking in her tub.

Savoring the moment, she closed her eyes and thought back to the book club meeting. She didn't know what had triggered her bit of fun with those people, but she sure as hell got unexpected reactions out of them. She hadn't met any of the club members before that evening, nor did she know about their past. That shot in the dark was a bit of mischief on her part, figuring that out of eight people, maybe one would have a dark secret. To her surprise, it had hit home with several of them. She had watched their expressions as she made the ridiculous accusation, expecting them to take it in their stride and possibly be amused.

Instead, what she saw in most of their faces was fear of being discovered. It was clear to her that these individuals had something to hide. She had not anticipated this outcome and it showed that it was easy to mess with people's minds. She may use that kind of approach in her current book.

She had had a gut feeling about Madame Maxine and as a consequence made that "change of gender" comment.

It had met its target. The woman had returned her gaze with undisputed rage in her eyes.

The bold guy had given her a calculating glance as if trying to determine whether or not she was on the level with her remarks. The petite teacher and also the younger woman had both been frightened, that was clear. She hadn't been able to make out Suzanne's face clearly, since her hostess sat immediately next to her, but the husband stayed pokerfaced, and the nurse seemed more angry than afraid.

The cop didn't appear to take her seriously and she now remembered his words, "You're playing a dangerous game, lady!" Was that a threat or a friendly warning? Nonsense, the man was just letting her know that he was aware of her bluff. It doesn't really matter what he meant, since I'll never see him or any of the group again, she thought.

Minutes later, the soothing bath had served its purpose and Katherine fell into a restful sleep, without the slightest worry.

Several book club members were not that lucky, anticipating trouble, since each assumed that the author's accusation was meant for him or her. One person took action straight away and followed Katherine home that night. It was easy to do so on the freeway, but after exiting on Wheatland Avenue and navigating the surface streets in a residential area, it became a bit tricky. There was little traffic at that time of the night and the individual made sure to keep a generous distance with the headlights dimmed.

As Katherine drove into her detached garage, the person following her turned the headlights completely off before getting to her address and parked at the curb, watching her come out of the car and walk over to her front entrance.

It was a moonless night, pitch dark, except for the porchlight above the door of the residence, illuminating the small area at the front entrance. The stalker paid keen attention to Katherine's movements as she inserted her key into the lock and entered, without so much as a glance at her surroundings. No alarm system seemed to exist - - at least, she did not inactivate one - - and there was no evidence of any surveillance camera.

The person watched as lights went on at floor level of the house and waited. Less than five minutes later, they were turned off and one of the upstairs rooms was lit and the blinds drawn close. Shortly afterwards, another light came on in the window of a smaller room adjacent to it.

Must be her bedroom and bathroom, the person in the parked car presumed. Apparently, she is taking her bedtime bath, like she told us she was in the habit of doing. For a split second the pursuer was tempted to take care of business right then and there, but shook off the urge. This was only an orientation trip to stake out the territory, in case action was needed. It was too soon after the meeting to silence her, which would look suspicious. Silencing may not even be necessary, since Katherine Scherrer had left it unclear who and what she meant with her accusation. If indeed she needed to be taken care of, some planning was indicated.

The person started the ignition and slowly drove away, not switching on the headlights until three houses farther down the street.

CHAPTER 5

Violet's insomnia was even worse than usual. This time her restlessness had nothing to do with worrying about Covid. Instead, she mulled over the author's last remark before the book club meeting came to an end. Could she have meant me? Violet asked herself. If so, will my past, which I've tried to forget for the last 10 years, come to haunt me all over again?

She shuddered as she thought back to the ugly trial. And yes, she was found "not guilty," but people had looked at her sideways, not being convinced of her innocence. The boy was only a freshman in high school and she had been a woman of 30. How could he be the aggressor and rape her when he claimed it was the other way around? There were plenty of people in that town in the Midwest who believed him, and not her.

Even her own husband had doubted her innocence. After trying to cope with his mistrust for a couple of years, she gave up and divorced him, and then had had no choice but to start a new life somewhere else.

Some of Katherine's words resonated with her over and over: "People can change their hair color and move to a different state, but I never forget a face, nor a voice." In Violet's former life she had been a brunette; now she was a blonde and lived in Southern California.

It was close to three o'clock in the morning before she finally fell into an exhausted sleep.

*****

Maxine Dupont, aka Madame Maxine, aka Max Dupont, was furious with the author for the allegation brought forward at the meeting. Sleep did also not come easy to her that night. The more she thought about it, the angrier she became. How dare that woman make the remark about altering one's gender? she thought. Sure, she had thrown in other stuff, like changing hair color, name, or weight, but that didn't fool me. Her accusation was aimed in my direction, she mused. Obviously, the author had been referring to that unfortunate incident a while back. But that was settled out of court. No way could Katherine Scherrer have known about it.

Maxine had carefully guarded that secret for a decade and wasn't about to have her livelihood ruined by that prying author. If by chance that meddling writer did get wind of what had happened when one of her clients misinterpreted her reading and had acted on it, it would be a disaster. Should that episode become public, her business would suffer. In her line of work, reputation meant everything.

The woman needs to be stopped, Maxine thought, before she destroys my livelihood.

She suddenly chuckled to herself and mused, I should have read her palm right then and there, telling her that she herself was in danger. That would have shut her up, I'm sure.

With that pleasant thought in mind, the psychic finally got some sleep.

*****

Luke Grey was watching the 11:00 p.m. news but could not concentrate on what he saw and heard. For the umpteenth time he was trying to figure out what had triggered the author's sudden change of mood at the book club meeting. The friendly conversation of discussing her current book, followed by questions and answers about how she approached her writing, had turned morbid. He tried to remember at which member she had looked at when making her accusation. Come to think of it, had she stared at him, or was that his imagination at work?

He was sure that they had been strangers until that night's meeting. So that bit of news she threw at them about never forgetting a face or voice could not apply to him. There had been an investigation but no one had been able to prove that he'd embezzled the money; he'd been too smart and careful. The case, if one could call it such, had never made it to the media. He had not even been fired, but decided to give notice. It was impossible that this woman knew him, or heard about his misappropriation of assets. Or could she have?

Now, so many years later, he owned his own business as a well-established financial advisor. His clientele ranged from average folks, for whom he prepared tax returns, to the wealthy, who trusted him with investing their capital. He had made a name for himself in the field and was known as a man with integrity. Although the statute of limitations for his crime had long expired, Katherine Scherrer could ruin it all for him with her gossip. He could not let that happen if indeed he was the author's target.

*****

At 26 years of age, Rosalia Acosta was the youngest member of the club and had no past to speak of. She was in her fourth year of working at the Los Angeles courts as a Spanish interpreter and loved her job. She had recently met a man, who could be "the one." In short, life was good. Yet that night she lay awake remembering the image of Yolanda being tossed in the air and landing face down on the asphalt with a thud.

It had happened in her senior year of high school. Her boyfriend had broken up with her and dated Yolanda, a girl with a reputation. Rosalia had been hurt but would have gotten over him in time. However, Yolanda was the type of girl who would brag about her newest victory and rub it in.

Rosalia walked home from school one day, minding her own business. When she passed a group of girls standing in a huddle, Yolanda suddenly broke loose from her friends, keeping in step with Rosalia, taunting her.

Yolanda bombarded Rosalia with a string of spiteful allegations, shouting profanities at her. The mocking and provocation continued while Rosalia stepped up her pace to almost running while the other did likewise, never shutting up.

Finally, Rosalia had had enough, yelling, "Get away from me!" giving the other girl a forceful shove, which pushed her off the sidewalk and into the street. At that exact instant a speeding car, unable to stop, rammed into Yolanda. The kid driving the car later told the police that the girl had jumped in front of his vehicle without warning. Yolanda survived but ended up with brain damage.

Rosalia thought, that became the accepted version: *she leaped into the street.* The boy was charged with speeding and reckless driving, but nobody saw me doing the pushing, and I kept silent about it. And the longer I waited, the less

I had the courage to tell the truth. It was an accident - - I didn't mean for her to get run over - - but I can't shake off the guilty feeling that will stay with me for the rest of my life.

She sat straight up in bed and wondered, can one be charged with manslaughter even if the person isn't killed? She had never thought about it before but felt that she needed to research the topic. Then she tried to figure out how Katherine Scherrer could possibly know what had really happened. Was she there that day, maybe walking behind them or across the street, she wondered. If so, why didn't she speak up right then and there? The whole thing didn't make sense. Maybe she meant someone else with her accusing remark. I sure had the feeling though that she was staring directly at me.

CHAPTER 6

Brian was sitting in the cockpit on his flight to Dallas Fort Worth. The ascent out of LAX and the gradual climb was behind him. He had broken through the clouds and had been cruising at a steady altitude for a stretch. He now nodded to the co-pilot and then put the plane into cruise control.

He relaxed, closed his eyes, and let his mind drift back to the book club meeting. Could the writer's allegation have been targeting him? he mused. Sure, bigamy was a crime but he had never looked at it as such. He tried to remember how it all started: meeting Lillian while stationed back East for a month, being attracted and falling in love. Before he knew what was happening, they were married, and three-quarters of a year later their daughter, Ali, was born. His only excuse was that at 42, he had been going through a midlife crisis.

After juggling his double life for eight years, it almost became routine. The stock market had been kind to him so far, enabling him to afford two households. The two women were different types. Suzanne was 5 foot 8 and a brunette, whereas Lillian was fair and barely reached his shoulders at 5 foot 3. He loved both his wives, his sons with Suzanne, and his daughter with Lillian. There was no way he would want to hurt any of them.

He had managed to create a second identity and had two different social security numbers, as well as a driver license for both states. In California, he was Brian Morlett, using the name he had been born with. To his family and friends on the East Coast, he was known as Bill Moran. As far as Suzanne knew, he stayed in an Airbnb when stationed in New York, but in reality he lived in an apartment with Lillian and Ali. Likewise, he had told Lillian that he shared a condominium with a fellow pilot when in Los Angeles. Neither woman had ever questioned the extra key on his keychain. They either had not noticed it or, if they had, were not curious.

Since the meeting had come to an end, he had racked his brain, trying to remember if he had ever come into contact with Katherine prior to her guest appearance at his house. He came up empty. However, it needed to be looked into more closely. There was no way he would let that woman ruin his life.

*****

Charlotte Chadwick had fallen into an exhausted sleep as soon as her head had hit the pillow that night. She was working 12-hour shifts at the hospital and the book club was the only recreational luxury she allowed herself these days. Even though she was a speed-reader, she lacked the time to read a book a month during the pandemic. Consequently, she had missed many meetings in the last two years.

Since it sounded interesting, she had made a special effort to read Katherine Scherrer's current mystery. She got out of the night shift that week and the next, so that she was able to attend the meeting.

Getting ready for work the following morning she thought, now I wish I hadn't been there. The author addressed eight people with her vague allegation. Why am I even ready to think she meant me by it? Nobody knows what I did, so why worry? And anyhow, my action was morally justified. There was no cure for the patient who begged me to pull the plug. I did so out of compassion, putting him out of his misery.

While brushing her teeth, Charlotte looked at herself in the mirror and said aloud, "You're a mess! Get a grip and forget about the woman and her agenda. Patients who need you are waiting in the ICU."

*****

Theo Oxley sat at a briefing at police headquarters, having trouble paying attention. Instead, he gave way to his own pondering. What the hell had that author talked about at the end of the meeting? No matter who she has in mind with her accusation, she plays a dangerous game. I hope she realizes that.

At first, the idea that she could have meant him with her remark had not entered his mind, but when leaving the Morlett residence, her warning that she never forgot a face, nor a *voice*, resonated. His face was average but his baritone voice had a unique tone.

Three years ago, he had been investigated for using excessive force during an arrest. The suspect in question had been hospitalized but later fully recovered. The investigation had been internal, within the Police Force, and Theo Oxley was found innocent of any wrongdoing.

Thinking back, he could have handled the suspect less aggressively, and nowadays, he conducted himself more humanely in similar situations. The idea that the woman had gotten wind of the incident was ridiculous, and he could not think of another occurrence that would point her finger in his direction. Should he give it a rest or investigate further?

Suddenly the other officers got to their feet and Theo realized that the briefing session was over.

CHAPTER 7

A couple of days later, Katherine received the first anonymous phone call. Not recognizing the caller's number, her first impulse was to ignore it, but then she changed her mind and took the call. The person on the line did not give his or her name and basically seemed to be fishing for information about what Katherine had hinted at the other night. She did not tell the person the truth and got a kick out of the caller's concern.

There were two more calls from different members of the book club, playing at the same cat-and-mouse game. Katherine was not the least bit scared or worried, but rather amused.

The last of those talks changed her attitude and went like this:

Caller: "Who did you have in mind with your accusation, and what do you know?"

Katherine: "Well, hello there! You're trying hard to alter your voice, but I do know who you are."

Caller: "Answer the question!"

Katherine: "I know what you did but don't worry. Your secret is safe with me."

Caller: "Are you trying to blackmail me?"

Katherine thought the idea was hilarious and laughed, deciding that it was time to let the person know that she had just had some fun with everyone on the night of the book club meeting. But she did not get the chance. Frustrated, the caller hung up as she laughed.

Katherine stared at the phone and thought, I have no idea who that was, but the person thinks that I do. And it looks like whoever made that call has something serious and damaging to hide. This is no longer fun and games. Should I be worried about my safety? I'll be careful when I'm out and about, she told herself.

The caller thought, she obviously knows and is even amused. How does the saying go? "He who laughs last laughs the loudest," or something like that. I'll teach her to make fun of me! She may not do anything about her knowledge by either blackmailing or going to the authorities, but I can't leave it up to chance. It sure smells of blackmail, though. A good thing I staked out her house and surroundings already and formed a plan in case it becomes necessary to silence her. All I have to do now is execute that plan as soon as I can.

CHAPTER 8

Katherine was soaking in her tub at 10:00 p.m. on Thursday, February 17, feeling good. She had long overcome her temporary writer's block and was "living" her story through each of her characters once again. She knew exactly where she was going with her plot and it promised to be an excellent one. As an author, she was back on track, and she had no complaints concerning her real life either. She smiled to herself when thinking about Caitlin's phone call on Valentine's Day. "I love you Grandma. Be my Valentine!"

As to that last anonymous phone call, several days had passed and nothing happened. She had watched her surroundings, making sure nobody followed her whenever she'd left her house. Now she was confident she wasn't in any danger but hoped that the person would call again, giving her a chance to explain. And yes, to apologize for playing her game and let the individual know that she did not know his or her secret, nor anybody else's.

But it was too late and she would never get that chance. Her adversary was parked at the curb in front of her house in the dark. The person had watched as the light at ground level was turned off and the upstairs ones came on, then delayed five more minutes to give her time to draw the bath, before jumping into action. Picking the lock was child's play, and the shoes came off and were left at the entrance.

Once inside, the antagonist heard music coming from the second floor, which was lucky because it would drown out any noise from his or her approach. The person waited at the foot of the stairs for a second and listened. Yes, there was the slight splashing of water.

Katherine reached for the wine glass, took another sip, and replaced it on the stool next to the bathtub. Then she closed her eyes and savored the moment. The sudden force that pushed her under the water made her open her eyes and want to scream, but she swallowed soapy water instead, and her attempt was nothing but a restrained gurgle. There was a momentary struggle, but the arms that held her under were too strong. The frantic twitching of her own arms and legs came to a halt as her body became limp and she lost consciousness.

The cleaning lady found her lifeless corpse the next morning. She dropped her mop and bucket of water and ran - - screaming at the top of her lungs - - down the street until a neighbor caught up with her.

The author's accidental drowning in her own bathtub was reported on the Friday evening news, as well as in the Saturday Los Angeles Times and other local papers.

CHAPTER 9

On Saturday evening, the Morletts sat facing one another across the table at their favorite Italian restaurant in Montrose. They had both ordered their customary dish of veal piccata and risotto.

While waiting for the food to be served, they held up their glasses of Chardonnay in a toast. Brian said, "Here's to a belated Valentine's Day!"

"Belated or not, this is better than a box of candy," Suzanne remarked, as they clicked their goblets.

They spoke little during the meal, savoring every bite. It was not until they lingered over espressos that they started to converse.

Brian reached over and touched her hand, saying, "I missed you, Suzanne."

"Same here. At what time did you make it in Thursday night? I didn't know when to expect you home and went to bed early."

"I don't remember, but you were already asleep and I didn't want to wake you." He added, "The good news is that, starting tomorrow, I'll be flying out of home base for an entire month."

"Out of Burbank! That is indeed good news." And after a moment of silence she remarked, "Isn't it awful about Katherine Scherrer?"

"Yes, her drowning in the bathtub was such a freak accident."

"I've been thinking - - -"

"It's dangerous when you think," he interrupted with a grin.

"Seriously, I want *you* to think about it. Katherine accused someone in our book club group of having a dark secret, or even of being a criminal, and the next week she is dead."

"What are you implying?"

"That she was murdered."

"Don't get carried away, Suzanne. That was a coincidence. She told us that she was in the habit of relaxing in her tub while drinking wine before going to bed. She obviously got drowsy, fell asleep, and slipped under the water. The bit in the paper mentioned that it was an accidental drowning and that no foul play was under investigation."

"I don't believe in coincidences of that kind. Yes, she told us about taking a bath every night and someone took advantage of that knowledge and killed her. If I'm right, then I'm at least partly responsible, since I invited her to the meeting in the first place."

"Neither you, nor anybody else, is to blame for her death. Don't torture yourself, and above all, don't get any ideas about playing detective," said Brian. "If by a slim chance you're right - - and I'm sure you're wrong - - keep out of it and let the authorities do their job."

The lovely evening out had suddenly ended on a less pleasant note. But the comment Brian had made about not getting involved made her put her imaginary foot down and she thought, I may have to do just that.

CHAPTER 10

Suzanne enjoyed Mondays, her day off at the library, which she had long reserved for doing volunteer work at the zoo. She would don her red polo shirt with the zoo logo and sturdy shoes and get there at 9:00 a.m., clocking in at the volunteer entry.

The zoo opened at 10:00 a.m., so there was plenty of time for docents to get their assignments from a chairperson, plus information about new animals joining the zoo, including their adaptations and adjustments to the new surroundings.

The roughly 60 acres of exhibits were organized according to the continents of the species' origins. There were two types of tours docents would be assigned to. Explaining the lives and habitat of trees and plants was one. The other was informing the audience of the origin, environment, habits, and adaptation of the animals.

Typically, Suzanne was assigned to take zoo enthusiasts on a tour of the animal exhibits, which would take about two to three hours, depending on her audience. With a class of kids, which was more customary during the week, the tour took usually two hours.

On Monday, February 21, she met a class of seventh graders at the gate and took them on an animal tour.

The stench of the flamingos was already strong before they spotted the beautiful pinkish-orange birds. One of the girls asked, "Do they smell bad because they like to stand so close together?"

"No, stupid," replied a boy, "it's because they fart."

Suzanne was used to smart aleck comments and said, "You are both wrong. Like all species, the flamingos have long adapted to their environment in order not to become extinct. Their diet of shrimp-based foods keeps their feathers the brilliant colors we enjoy looking at. Their feathers would in fact be gray if they didn't consume shrimp. So they smell that way because of the food they eat."

And she elaborated, "In the olden days, there used to be feather hunters, who would travel to exotic islands to collect flamingo plumes for adorning ladies' hats. By the time their ships arrived in cities like New York, for example, the feathers had long turned gray."

They toured around the large elephant exhibit, where there was plenty of room for the animals to roam. Suzanne explained, "Throughout the entire zoo, the terrain and habitation is fine-tuned to each creature's original environment. No animal is caged, and a lot of thought and care is taken to make their new surroundings as authentic as their settings in the wild."

Some of the kids complained, not liking the steep terrain Suzanne made them climb to the most northern part of the zoo. On the way downhill, as they stopped at the giraffes' habitat and observed an animal eat from the very top of a branch, one exclaimed, "Look at the funny color of its tongue!"

Suzanne said. "That's a Masai giraffe. His tongue is purple and 18 inches long! The reason for the color is a built-in sunscreen. The giraffes' tongues are so long and constantly exposed to the sun that nature provided for natural protection."

And a little farther down, she pointed at the gerenuk exhibit and said, "And here is another interesting animal. It lives in Africa and can stand on its hind legs, adapting to its environment. The gerenuk has similarities with the giraffe but of course is much smaller. The giraffe eats from the topmost of a tree, whereas the gerenuk stands on his hind legs to reach and browse the middle part of it."

One of the animals was doing so at that very moment, and the kids watched food go down his long, skinny neck and then come back up. The animal chewed again, and back down it went once more. This happened several times in a row, back and forth, like an elevator.

The teens complained again as they hiked back up the steep incline but were happy to be dropped off at the children's play area for lunch, where Suzanne said good-bye to them.

She loved it all, but on that particular Monday, it became routine as her mind went somewhere else. Walking by the zebra exhibit on her way out of the zoo, she was reminded of that day in December when she had recognized the author and stopped to talk with her. Now she wished that she had not. The more she thought about what had happened to Katherine, the more convinced she became that her death was no accident.

And to her shock and horror, during the previous night, she had experienced a nightmare about her sister's drowning, which used to happen often during her teenage years. The nightmares had stopped decades ago, so why did she have that terrible dream now?

Not for the first time she pictured each book club member as a possible culprit. What did she really know about any of them? Not much, she admitted to herself. She thought back to the beginning of the club, four years prior. Violet had been a regular at the library, checking out a book at least once a month. One day she suggested that she'd welcome a book club. Suzanne thought it was a great idea and posted a flyer at the library's bulletin board, and so the book club came into being. Before the pandemic, it was held at the library. Some members came and went, but most of the current group had been there from the beginning.

Two years ago, Theo Oxley replaced his wife, who had been a devoted member until she passed away. At first, he did so out of loyalty to her, since that had been her wish, but it was obvious that he had warmed up to reading and discussing books. Every so often he would sit one out if it was too "girly" of a read, according to him. Early on, while in mourning, he had been on the quiet side, but as time went by, he had found his way back to his dry humored self.

Violet was the only one of the group of people whom she knew more about. They were not exactly best friends but met for lunch or coffee once in a blue moon. The idea that the genteel teacher could commit a crime, let alone murder, was absurd. Yet, Suzanne thought, if I want to get results, I can't exclude anyone. Brian told me to leave it alone, but I owe it to Katherine to get justice.

Naturally, she could not alert the authorities before she had something to show for her allegation. They wanted facts, not some woman's gut feeling. She needed to search out those facts and determine who the culprit was before she could even consider going to the police.

By the time Suzanne was done with her tour, passed the exit gate, and walked to where her car was parked, she had formed a plan about how to proceed.

On that same evening, she composed a group e-mail to the book club members. She wrote several drafts, as she felt that choosing the right wording was essential. She ended up sending the following, hoping that she had captured the right tone:

"Hello all,

"Everyone left in a hurry the other night. We did not even take the time to vote on which book we should read for the April meeting. We need to do that now. The list of potential authors and their titles is attached.

"And now to a more somber matter. I'm sure you are all aware of the sad news about Katherine Scherrer. I am having a hard time dealing with her sudden death, and I feel somewhat responsible and need to talk with each of you in private.

"I'll keep in touch to make arrangements.

"Best,

"Suzanne"

CHAPTER 11

A get-together with Violet had been overdue, so Suzanne suggested they meet the next day. During her lunch break, she walked over to their favorite Montrose hangout, a block away from the library. It was a relatively warm day and they chose the restaurant's outdoor seating, which they preferred since the start of Covid.

Suzanne swallowed the last bite of her sandwich and then said, "You've been eyeing me with an angry expression from the moment we sat down. What gives?"

"Yes, I'm angry at you, and hurt. I almost stood you up, but then I decided to confront you instead. What I told you was in strict confidence. You had no right to pass it on to the author," Violet shot back.

"What are you talking about?"

"I opened up to you about my past during a vulnerable moment and you exploited it."

It took Suzanne a moment to grasp what the other meant. "Oh, you mean what that boy did to you and then what he accused you of?"

Violet's reproachful stare was enough of an answer.

"I did not tell that to anybody and certainly not to Katherine Scherrer. What made you think I did?"

And before the teacher had a chance to respond, she answered her own question. "I see. You think Katherine meant you with her accusation. That's absurd. You were found not guilty."

"Yes, I was, but plenty of people still believed the boy's version. Even my own husband wasn't a hundred percent sure of my innocence. Why do you think I never remarried?"

Suzanne shrugged her shoulders.

"I don't know if I can ever trust anyone again, that's why."

A couple of high school kids walking by on the sidewalk looked over to their table and yelled, "Hello, Ms. Richards!"

Violet nodded to them. Then she looked at her watch and said, "I have an afternoon class."

"We'd better hurry up with our talk, then. I doubt very much that Katherine was pointing the finger at you, and if she did, she must have learned about your past from someone else." She took a sip of water, then continued, "Now let me get to what we really need to discuss. I suspect that our lady author was murdered, and - - -"

"Wait a minute. I read in the paper that she had accidentally drowned in her bathtub."

"Sure, but think about it. She makes her accusation and days later she dies. We all knew that she was in the habit of taking a bath at bedtime. She said so herself at the meeting."

There was a sudden alertness in Violet's eyes as she said, "You think a book club member killed her?"

"That stands to reason. I need to narrow it down, though. I'm trying to uncover secrets that some may have and inquire into alibis of the night in question."

"What qualifies you to do that?"

"Nothing, but I feel responsible since I invited her to our meeting. The authorities will want proof, or at least a plausible motive. I presume that Katherine took her bath between 10:00 and 11:00 at night. This is strictly routine but I need to ask everyone. Where were you last Thursday night from, let's say, 9:45 until 11:15?"

Violet said, "I resent that question."

"I need to inquire into alibis. I can't make an exception with you."

"I was home. And you know good and well that I live alone and have nobody that can vouch for me."

"I believe you, but had to ask. Now to the others. Do you happen to know of any secret past anyone in our group might have?"

Violet shook her head. Then she said "Oh!"

"You remember something?"

"No, it's just a thought that popped into my head when Katherine talked about never forgetting someone even if they changed their gender." She seemed a bit embarrassed and went on, "Did you ever notice Maxine's hands?"

"What about them?"

"They are huge. And so are her feet. She must wear a size 11 shoe. While the author was talking, I thought it possible that Maxine could have been male to begin with."

Suzanne said, "That never occurred to me. And anyhow, her gender has nothing to do with what I'm trying to find out."

Violet stated, "I'm giving you a piece of advice. Don't get involved and leave the detecting to the authorities."

Then she checked the time again and said, "I've got to run."

As she reached for her wallet to pay her share of the bill, Suzanne stopped her, saying, "Lunch is on me. I've made you suffer enough."

Left by herself, Suzanne took a notebook out of her purse. She had made a list of seven names. She now wrote next to Violet's: *Very weak motive concerning a rape case of 10 years ago. As to alibi, she claimed to have been at home alone.*

CHAPTER 12

On her walk back to the library, Suzanne reflected on her next move. The talk with the teacher had given her an idea about how to approach the rest of the group. Violet had jumped to the conclusion that she had leaked the bit about her past to Katherine. That made her think, what if I pretend that the author had disclosed whom she meant with her comment and had even given me details? Surely that would stir things up and the guilty person would take the bait. I'll run it by Brian and see what he makes of the idea, she concluded.

Warren went to band practice after dinner on that Tuesday evening, so Suzanne had Brian to herself. She remarked, "Did I tell you that I'm thrilled you're flying in and out of Burbank these days?"

"More than once!"

Then she jumped right to what was foremost on her mind and said, "I've decided to poke around and discover who could have murdered Katherine Scherrer."

He shook his head and stated, "Bad idea! But knowing you, there is nothing I can say to make you change your mind, so I won't even try. I wish I could stop you from playing detective but since I can't, remember the cop's judgement that the writer was playing a dangerous game. That goes for you too. So be extremely careful!"

"Don't worry, I'm capable of watching my back."

She then explained how she planned to tackle each person and then said, "Since I'm new at this, I need to rehearse my performance. Let me practice on you."

He humored her and replied, "Sure, go ahead."

"Where were you on Thursday, February 17, from about 9:45 p.m. until 11:15 p.m.?"

He replied, "I was driving home from LAX and arrived at my house at 10:30."

"Do you have anyone who can verify that?"

"I taxied in at LAX from my New York flight at 9:10, which is on my record. I did not time myself going through the airport red tape, nor when I started my car, but traffic was relatively light and I got home at approximately 10:30." He winked at her and added, "My wife can attest to that."

Suzanne gave him a meaningful glance as she stated, "Katherine took me into her confidence. You see, I know whom she targeted with her remark, and what's more, the guilty secret that's involved."

Not getting a reaction from Brian, she continued, "Your transgression dates way back, before we were even married but that doesn't mean it's irrelevant."

Inwardly, her husband sighed with relief. To her face, he chuckled and remarked, "You mean old sins have long shadows?"

"Don't make fun of me. Granted, my tactic does not work with you, since you're not the guilty party. But don't you think it will scare the real criminal?"

"I hope it does not scare the person enough to take action as he or she did with the writer. That's if you are correct with your idea that she was murdered, which I don't believe for a moment. Like I said from the beginning, leave it alone. Even if you should be right and get lucky - - or rather unlucky - - and discover the culprit, it will not bring Katherine back but will put you in danger."

"I told you before, I can take care of myself."

Brian insisted, "This entire exercise is pointless. The lady drowned in her tub by accident. No matter how much bait you throw at the book club members, you won't get results, because there is no guilty person."

That said, the subject was closed for him and he turned on the TV.

CHAPTER 13

Charlotte Chadwick was back to the long night shift at the hospital. When the phone woke her up out of a deep sleep on Wednesday at 12:00 noon, she was miffed. She let it go to voicemail, thinking it was a telemarketing call. Nobody close to her dared to call in the middle of the day when she had the night shift, unless it was an emergency.

Only half awake, she listened to the message, *"Hi Charlotte, this is Suzanne. Looks like I did not catch you at home. As explained in my e-mail, I'd like to get together with you. When is a good time and place? Let me - - -"*

Charlotte initially was going to ignore the call but changed her mind, deciding it would look bad if she didn't talk with the woman. She interrupted the recording, saying, "I'm here."

Hearing the other's groggy voice, Suzanne said, "Oh, so sorry for waking you up! I can call back."

"That's okay," Charlotte replied, already becoming fully alert. She thought to herself, no need to get her husband involved, nor the kids.

Aloud she said, "I don't have time to meet you anyplace sometime soon, but if you come to my house tomorrow at 5:00 p.m., I have a few minutes before getting ready for work. I'll be able to give you my full attention; my husband won't be home yet, our daughter has Girl Scouts, and our son will be at karate practice."

Suzanne said, "Perfect! I can leave the library a few minutes early. See you tomorrow."

All book club members lived in the Glendale, Montrose, or La Crescenta area. Charlotte's house was only a couple of blocks away from the library. Suzanne showed up promptly at 5:00 p.m. on Thursday, February 24.

Aware that her interview time was limited, she came straight to the point and said, "Katherine confided in me. I know whom and what she meant."

"You're bluffing. Why are you doing this?"

"I think you know," Suzanne said, pinning her with a meaningful glance.

"She accidently drowned while taking a bath. It happens! If you're suggesting anything else, you're fishing for gory sensationalism."

"Katherine was afraid and wished that she had not made those comments at the book club meeting. She told me so a few days later and, sure enough, shortly afterwards she died."

Charlotte said, "I see. She told you about the phone call."

Getting no response, she continued, "It was stupid of me to call. I realized that as soon as I hung up, but I needed to know that she did not mean me with her accusation. I didn't accomplish anything with the call, however. On the contrary, she treated it as a joke and guessed that it was me, even though I disguised my voice. But she certainly was not afraid and did not seem threatened!"

"No matter what you say, she knew of someone's dark past and was silenced because of that knowledge."

Charlotte pointed a finger at Suzanne for emphasis and said, "Just so you know, I wasn't the only one who called her. Katherine made some kind of a remark that her line seemed to be buzzing with anxious club members." And she raised her voice and added, "Even if you are right, you don't know who it is. Like I said before, you're bluffing. Katherine did not tell you who she meant."

"Regardless, I owe it to her to look into it. Tell me where you were on Thursday, February 17, from 9:45 p.m. until 11:15 p.m."

"I take offense to your scrutiny of me, but let me think. The 17th was exactly one week ago. I had the day shift then and was home all evening, going to bed at 11:00. Does that satisfy your curiosity?"

"Any witnesses?"

"My husband can vouch for me, but I'd prefer to leave him out of it."

Charlotte made a point of looking at her wrist watch and Suzanne knew her time was up. Already at the door she said, "Oh, don't forget to send me an e-mail with your choice of book for our April read."

"I'm withholding my vote as I doubt whether I'll have any leisure time in the near future. And anyhow, I'm debating quitting the book club altogether."

"I'd hate to lose you but I do understand. Nurses are worked to the bone these days, and I appreciate all you sacrifice."

While walking to her car she thought, I really offended her. And if she is innocent, I'm truly sorry. I didn't learn much from the interview but the bit that more people seemed to have been worried enough to make an inquisitive call to Katherine is interesting.

Once home, she went in search of her notebook. Next to Charlotte's name she wrote: *No known motive, but the fact that she made that probing call to Katherine indicates that she has a dark secret. As to alibi, she claimed to have been at home. No doubt her husband will verify it. Can one trust a spouse's confirmation?*

CHAPTER 14

Luke Grey did not want Suzanne to come to his office in Pasadena, as he was not in the mood to explain her visit to his associate nor his secretary. He also did not invite her to his home in Montrose. He grudgingly agreed to meet at her house on Friday evening.

Suzanne tried to sum up what she knew about each person before his or her interview. In Luke Grey's case that did not amount to much. She knew that he was divorced. When he first joined the club, he had mentioned something about his ex-wife, but she had forgotten what that was. Trying to remember now was no good; she came up empty.

When Luke arrived at Suzanne's home, he was greeted at the front door by Brian, who was on his way out.

"Sorry! I can't stop Suzanne from interrogating everyone. Your best bet is to humor her and play along," Brian said as he walked to his car.

Luke made a thumbs-up gesture and entered, not sure what the other meant.

Suzanne settled him in a dining room chair with a cup of coffee and said, "I heard that. It's not so bad. The three members I interviewed already survived the scrutiny."

Ignoring her comment, Luke asked, "What are you up to? Based on your e-mail notice and your phone call to schedule this meeting, I assumed it had to do with a memorial service for Katherine or maybe a monetary contribution, since you wanted to talk with us individually. So, what gives?"

"I'm sure you can guess!"

"Are you suggesting that Katherine's death was not an accident?"

"You've got that right. I don't believe in coincidences. And since you are a smart guy, I'm positive the thought has crossed your mind too."

"According to the authorities, she drowned in her own tub by accident. I'm sure they checked any other possibility, like forceful entry by a stranger, or any sign of a struggle, and so forth, before they came to that conclusion."

"But they don't know about her accusation of only a week before," Suzanne shot back. And she added, "Would it surprise you to know that Katherine confided in me?"

He shrugged and said, "Not really. But if so, you would have gone to the police with your knowledge, the good citizen that you are."

"Oh, I will. As soon as I'll have a little more to offer them. Brian thinks I should leave it alone, but I feel responsible for what happened, since I invited her to the book club meeting in the first place."

"I think he's right. Playing detective could be dangerous."

"I can handle myself," she said. "I hope you don't mind answering my simple alibi question I'm posing to everybody. Where were you on Thursday, February 17, from 9:45 p.m. until 11:15 p.m.?"

"Like Brian suggested, I will humor you and answer. I was home on that Thursday evening, like most nights, during the time you mentioned. At 11 o'clock I watched the news. Since I live alone, you'll have to take my word for it."

Luke was drinking the last few sips of his coffee, and as she was watching him do so, she suddenly remembered what he had said about his ex-wife, years ago. His remark had been that paying alimony to his wife was a lot cheaper than supporting her high maintenance lifestyle.

It gave her an idea and she remarked, "Now that we're done with business, how is life treating you these days? I assume that your ex has remarried and you're released from paying alimony."

He belted out a sarcastic laugh and replied, "I wish! Narissa is shacking up these days and will most likely never remarry. Why should she when a monthly check from me comes in without her having to lift a finger? And what's frustrating is that she makes more than enough to support herself as a real estate agent but it looks like she'll hang on to my wallet for life."

Realizing she had touched a sore spot, Suzanne ended the interview and thanked him for e-mailing his choice of author and book title for the club's April read.

As soon as Luke left, she wrote next to his name in her notebook: *No known motive, but he clearly does not want me to investigate. As to alibi, he is another person who claims to have been home alone.*

She tucked the notebook away and thought, I'm glad he mentioned his ex-wife's name. It should be easy to find a realtor by the name of Narissa Grey. Who knows, maybe the woman will be willing to talk about Luke's past.

CHAPTER 15

Brian was not due home until late Sunday night. Warren, their youngest son, had been invited to an overnight at Big Bear where his friend's family owned a cabin and the boys took advantage of two days of skiing while the local snow lasted.

As a result, Suzanne had the weekend to herself and determined to make an adventure of it. Meeting Madame Maxine on her own turf would be a new experience for her.

She opted to come unannounced on Saturday afternoon. The bell overhead chimed as she opened the door. Stepping inside the psychic's dimmed shop after leaving the bright outdoors, she was slightly disoriented as her eyes got adjusted to the darkness. The heavy curtains were drawn shut and the only light came from a one-bulb lamp shining directly onto a round wooden table. At first, she could barely make out the shape of Madame Maxine, who sat in semi-darkness behind the table.

"Come on in, my dear, and close the door behind you."

As Suzanne took a few steps toward the table in the center of the small room, the other's tone of voice was no longer inviting as she said, "Oh, it's you!"

"Yes, it's me. As I let you know in my e-mail, we need to talk." With an embarrassed smile she added, "But first, I'm curious what a session with a psychic is like, so treat me as you would a client."

Maxine's sense of business kicked in and she replied, "No problem, but you need to pay for my service. I charge $250 an hour."

"Fair enough."

Maxine's mannerism suddenly became extremely foreign as she said, "A tarot card reading, or would the lady prefer to extend her palm so I may tell her fortune?"

Suzanne chose the tarot cards, and so Madame Maxine reached for the deck and presented a spread, saying, "I'll do the Celtic Cross spread." And she ordered, "Run your hand over the spread and then choose one card."

Suzanne did so and turned the card right side up. It was the *Fool* card. Maxine started the cross by placing that card at its center. Next, she gathered the rest of the cards, shuffled them, and then drew them from the deck, one at a time. The second card she drew was the *High Priestess*, which she placed crosswise over the *Fool*. The following cards she positioned around the two center cards in order of north, south, west, and east, making up the cross. Then she placed four more cards in a column to the right of the cross.

Before starting to analyze each card, Maxine stared at Suzanne in a probing way. The latter had no idea what was expected of her and stared back.

"You need to tell me what you want to know!"

"Oh, sure," said Suzanne. "My question is: can I solve the mystery I'm faced with?"

Madame Maxine stayed silent for what seemed like an eternity, scrutinizing the tarot cards with half-closed eyes. Then she announced the meaning of each picture card. She tapped the *Fool* with her finger and proclaimed, "Challenging decisions lie ahead involving risk." Looking at the *High Priestess* card she said, "Don't always trust your gut."

She interpreted the rest of the eight cards with great flair and drama in her voice, keeping her eyes half closed, and made the following comments:

"*Lovers* – Avoid making hasty decisions.

Tower – This is a dark card; the forebearer of a traumatic event.

Moon – I see an unexpected change of course.

Sun – You may accomplish what you seek but not without sacrifice.

Star – There is hope.

Death – You know what that card means and whom it refers to. Be on your guard.

World – Against all odds, you may accomplish your task.

Pointing to the last card, *Wheel of Fortune,* she warned, "You are at the mercy of fate, don't tempt it!"

Maxine came out of what had seemed like a trance. Then she opened her eyes wide and her voice took on a normal tone as she said, "My cards don't lie, so heed their warning."

Suzanne was a skeptic in regards to psychics but she was impressed with Madame Maxine's showmanship. The woman had stage talent, no doubt. Still, the dark, small room was claustrophobic and Suzanne thought, I had better get to the real reason I came here before I suffocate.

While writing a check and handing it over she said, "I'm sure you guessed what my talk with you is going to be about."

Maxine remarked, "I read your e-mail and it does not take psychic powers to put two and two together."

"Then you agree that Katherine Scherrer's drowning was not accidental."

"Maybe and maybe not. But it is not your place to find out. Like my tarot cards warned you, don't tempt fate! You will regret it if you do."

"I plan to get justice for Katherine. What would you say if I told you that she confided in me?"

"Hogwash!"

Suzanne glanced at the other's large hands and said, "Whom do you think Katherine meant with her transgender remark?"

There was malice in the psychic's eyes as she hissed, "Changing one's gender is not a crime."

"Agreed. So I'm sure you don't mind telling me where you were on Thursday, February 17, from 9:45 p.m. until 11.15 p.m."

Maxine consulted her phone calendar and then stated, "On that night I was the medium for a séance I held right here in my shop. As I remember, it was a long session. We started at 9:00 and it lasted until close to 11:00. I didn't look at the time when everyone left."

"Do you have people to verify that?"

"Sure, there were four of us," and she mentioned three names. "I cannot give you their contact information until I ask permission."

"Please do and then get back to me."

Suzanne got up to leave. She was already at the door when Maxine warned her again that no good would come from her pursuit. On the way to her car she thought, that was an interesting experience and an expensive way of gathering information. Was that bit about tempting fate a threat? she wondered.

Minutes later Madame Maxine made three phone calls, convincing each person that the séance had taken place on Thursday, February 17, and not on Friday the 18th, as they had formerly thought.

Suzanne was in church on Sunday, trying to concentrate on the priest's sermon without success, when it hit her. Like the psychic had said, changing one's gender was not a crime. But, Maxine had shown definite hostility when I questioned her. The woman must have a dark secret to keep and is determined not to let anyone find out about it, Suzanne determined. She wished she were a detective with access to records. She would run it by Brian, maybe he would come up with suggestions.

The congregation got to their feet, and she realized that the sermon was over and did likewise.

CHAPTER 16

After a bit of research, Suzanne located Narissa Grey as agent for an Orange County real-estate company. There was an open house in Seal Beach with Ms. Grey listed as the realtor on Sunday afternoon. The property was a single-family home, two blocks from the ocean, with an asking price of $1,200,000. After a quick bite for lunch, Suzanne got on her way.

Traffic was heavy on the 605 Freeway, which suited her fine. The open house was from noon to 3:00 p.m. and she wanted to arrive at its tail end, so that she could quiz the woman in private. She rolled into town at 2:20, found parking on a side alley near Main Street, and walked to the pier, passing charming boutiques and restaurants. She was not the only person out for a stroll on this mild and sunny Sunday afternoon in February. The little town was packed full of folks enjoying an outing.

From the pier she walked a couple blocks west and then a short distance in the direction away from the ocean, arriving at the open house a few minutes before three o' clock.

Narissa was greeting people by the entrance and stood up from behind a folding table as each newcomer appeared. Suzanne recognized her right away. The woman was even more striking than in the real estate picture ad, flawless from top to bottom. Her light brunette hair framed her face in a flattering style, and she had an impeccable French manicure. The skirt of her Giorgio Armani suit reached just above the knee, which drew attention to her perfect figure, and the three-inch pumps showed off her shapely legs. Luke's remark came to mind about his ex-wife being a high maintenance type of woman.

She smiled and said, "Hi there! I'm Narissa Grey. Feel free to look around and I'll be happy to answer any questions you may have."

Suzanne made the obligatory tour of the house. There was nothing remarkable she could see about the 3-bedroom, 1 ½ bath place. There was a good-size living room, but the kitchen was tiny. The reason this home was on the market for over a million dollars was because it was located close to the beach. Suzanne went out to the master bedroom balcony on the upper floor and, between buildings, got a glimpse of the ocean. Up there she waited until the last of the prospective buyers had left.

When she came down the stairs, the realtor was gathering the leftover brochures, disassembling the folding table, and straightening up the folding chair.

Suzanne looked at her watch and remarked, "It's already three o'clock. Sorry to make you work overtime."

The other smiled and replied, "I don't mind. Accommodating people goes with my job. Do you have any questions?"

"Not about the house; that's all self-explanatory. I'll give my husband the details and he may want to see it too. I'm just curious, are you by chance related to Luke Grey?"

"I was. Luke is my ex. You know him well?"

"Not really. We're both members of the same book club."

Narissa burst out laughing.

"What's so funny?"

"Luke must have changed! When I knew him, he never read any books." She laughed again and added, "Unless they were investment pamphlets."

Suzanne commented, "When he first joined the club, he mentioned needing a break from staring at numbers." She giggled and went on, "He also seemed unhappy about having to pay alimony."

Narissa was amused again and said, "That's what he calls it? I guess officially, that's what it is, but I prefer to think of it as hush money."

"What do you mean?"

"Nothing specific. I know he's Mr. Integrity now, but he wasn't years ago when I was married to him."

"Fascinating."

This time it was Narissa who checked the time and Suzanne quickly said, "I don't want to keep you here any longer."

The realtor handed her a brochure and said, "If your husband is interested, I'll be happy to give a private tour." And she added, "Give my regards to intellectual Luke!"

Suzanne heard the other's high-pitched laugh behind her, as she stepped outside.

CHAPTER 17

At the Morlett residence things did not go smoothly on Monday morning, February 28. Suzanne had a hard time getting her son up and ready for school, as he had come back late from his ski trip the night before. After knocking at Warren's door twice while yelling he was late getting up, without result, she finally burst into his room and pulled the comforter away from him. Fifteen minutes later, he left without having ate breakfast.

Brian had the day off and was sleeping in. When Suzanne was ready to leave, she peeked into the master bedroom.

"Oh, you're awake," she said and stepped closer.

"Come back to bed with me!"

"I'll take a raincheck. I'm due at the zoo soon, but have a quick question. Any suggestion on how I can get hold of suspects' criminal records?"

"You call your book club members suspects? Think of what you're saying. As far as we know, Katherine died by accident and you're not dealing with criminals. Give it a rest, already!"

"I've got to run. We'll pick this conversation up later," she replied, bent down to kiss him goodbye, and was out the door just as his cellphone rang.

Brian recognized the number and sighed with relief as he heard the front door bang shut, and answered the call.

"Hi Hon," said Lillian. "This is not an emergency, and I know you don't like me to call, but our daughter can't wait until you contact us. Here she is."

Seven-year-old Ali said, "Hi Daddy! Can you come to my dance recital? It's at two o'clock on Saturday, April 2."

"Hi, sweetie. Thanks for inviting me. I'll have to look at my schedule. I'll call you later today. I promise."

"When are you flying the East Coast route?"

"Soon."

"Miss you, Daddy!"

"I miss you too, Ali."

As soon as he ended the call, Brian thought, that was too close for comfort. If she'd have phoned a few seconds earlier, Suzanne would've still been in the room. He had told Lillian from the beginning, with the exception of an emergency, she should not ring him but always wait for his call, claiming that he could not be bothered while flying. He made sure to check with her at least every other day and so far, she had kept to her side of the bargain with few allowances over the years.

He shook his head and reflected that today's phone call could have been a disaster. He had been lucky for so many years. Both Suzanne and Lillian were trusting souls and sometimes he was amazed that he was able to pull off his double life. But now was not the time to have it all fall apart. When he'd phone Lillian and Ali back, he needed to be firm that calling him was not an option.

Then his mind switched to Suzanne, who was determined to play detective. So far, she was not dwelling on him with her interrogation, but sooner or later she may get it into her head to scrutinize his comings and goings. I can't let that happen, he thought.

.

CHAPTER 18

Rosalia Acosta had initially been worried when she read Suzanne's group e-mail, but since more than a week had passed without another word from the librarian about that private talk, she relaxed, thinking that the woman had changed her mind.

When Suzanne called on Tuesday, March 1, she realized that she was not off the hook yet.

The phone conversation went like this:

Suzanne: "Thanks for sending in your vote for our April read. I'm in possession of all the votes, and your book pick won. Now for the other matter, when would be a good day and time for us to get together?"

Rosalia: "What other matter?"

Suzanne: "We need to discuss Katherine Scherrer's death. I'm sure you know what I mean."

Rosalia: "I'm swamped at my job right now."

Suzanne: "You work at the courthouse downtown, right?"

Rosalia: "Correct."

Suzanne: "I can take a sick day anytime I want this week. How about meeting me at Philippe's during your lunch break? You choose the day."

Rosalia: "I might as well get it over with. Let's make it tomorrow, then."

After hanging up, Rosalia could have kicked herself. Why was she such a wimp? she wondered. She did not owe Suzanne anything. Why didn't she have the guts to say, "No. I don't want to get together to discuss Katherine's death." That would have been the answer anyone with a little backbone would have given.

She mused further, first the author made vague remarks about someone in the book club having committed a crime, bringing my guilty past to my mind. A past that I've been trying hard to forget. I didn't even know whether she meant me or somebody else. I should never have called her as nothing was accomplished with that call. Katherine Scherrer did not let on whom she meant. I realize that, if there should ever be an investigation, my phone records will show that I called the woman.

Rosalia's final thought was, I was so relieved to read in the newspaper that the writer's drowning was accidental. And now Suzanne is poking her nose into things. That can't turn out good.

CHAPTER 19

Suzanne had not been to downtown Los Angeles for years and decided to combine the interview with a little excursion, taking the train. On Wednesday morning, she drove to Pasadena and boarded the Metro Gold Line to Union Station. She exited the grandiose station at Alameda and walked over to Olvera Street, where she enjoyed a leisurely stroll along vendor stands, displaying piñatas, sombreros, serapes, pottery, leather goods, and traditional Mexican dresses.

Passing a restaurant where she and Brian had relished authentic *oaxaqueño* cuisine on a few occasions, she pondered that this was the first time she was touring downtown by herself.

She headed north on Broadway and walked under the golden dragon gateway that marked the entrance to Chinatown. Compared with other major cities, it was small, consisting of half a dozen restaurants, herbal shops, bakeries and souvenir stores. At the Central Plaza, the most popular tourist attractions were the wishing well and a statue of Bruce Lee.

Suzanne turned back south and walked along Broadway. At Temple, she checked her watch and decided not to take the time to hike up to the Cathedral of Our Lady of the Angels. Instead, she continued south on Hill Street, passing several court buildings. She walked among the homeless as well as lawyers in three-piece suits, pulling their documents along in dollies, then stood at the bottom of Angels Flight, the famous funicular.

Across the street, she stepped into the covered Grand Central Market, where the aromas of imported cheeses, meats, and fish hit her nostrils. She had entered the market on Hill Street and exited it on Broadway, then kept walking south on Broadway, which was lined with one bridal store after another.

At 7th Street she reached the jewelry district. The entire area was abundant with jewelry retail stores, stretching over several blocks, some in sizable merchant buildings with individual stall spaces rented out to jewelry dealers. Suzanne went inside one of the larger buildings. The array of sparkling gold, silver, diamond, and other precious stone jewelry displayed by so many merchants, all under one roof, was blinding.

She remembered when Brian took her shopping there for white gold diamond-cut hoop earrings, several years back. She suddenly missed his company, thinking it would be nice if he'd had time to accompany her on this outing. Then she reminded herself that the purpose of her being downtown was to interview Rosalia.

Brian would have never joined her, even if he'd been in town. She mused, why was he so against her investigating Katherine's death? He must really think I'm putting myself in danger. But no, he believes that her passing was an unfortunate accident. His worrying about my safety makes no sense.

She shook her head and thought, I need some fresh air; all the glitz and the bright lighting in here is making me dizzy.

It was time to make her way back in the direction she had come from. She took 3rd Street via Little Tokyo, passing by the Friendship Knot sculpture in a plaza of shops and restaurants with colorful paper lanterns strung overhead. Then she made her way to Alameda Street, the road that would bring her to Philippe's.

CHAPTER 20

Philippe's was one of the oldest restaurants in Los Angeles, famous for their French dip sandwiches. There was a rustic feeling about the place, with dark wood walls and sawdust scattered on the floor.

The two women arrived simultaneously. They made a contrasting pair, with Rosalia in a tailored business suit and Suzanne in leggings and a t-shirt. They ordered their French dips and freshly brewed iced teas at the counter, and then carried the food and drinks to one of the large communal tables. The place was busy but nobody paid attention to their conversation, as people were preoccupied with their own agendas while having lunch before returning to their jobs.

They had barely started eating when Rosalia jumped to the offensive before Suzanne had a chance to ease into the interview. The court interpreter said, "Why are you doing this? Are you getting a kick out of scaring me?"

"I see you realize what's at stake," Suzanne replied. "And to answer your question, I'm not out to get you but owe it to Katherine to learn the truth. She deserves justice."

"What makes you the judge? You have no legal standing, having no ties to either the legislative or executive branch. Heck, you're not even a private eye!"

Suzanne kept her calm despite the other's heated argument. She stated, "Katherine and I kept in touch after the book club meeting and before her death. She was frightened." And taking a shot in the dark, she added, "The phone call you made did not help matters."

"God, I wish I hadn't called! I swear I didn't threaten her. All I wanted to find out was who she'd meant with her accusation. I disguised my voice and didn't even think she knew it was me."

"Apparently, she did and seemed to know about that dark side in your past."

At that point Rosalia broke down crying and said, "It was an accident. I didn't mean to push her into the street." And she went on to confess her entire sad story about that fateful day during high school, when she got herself into the fight with Yolanda.

She ended with, "I should have come forward and told the authorities what happened, but I was too much of a coward. I can't imagine how Katherine got wind of it, but she must have thought that I pushed Yolanda in front of the speeding car on purpose."

She bit her lip, then placed her hand over her heart and stated, "I had nothing to do with the author's death. I swear to it."

"In that case, you don't mind telling me where you were on Thursday, February 17, from 9:45 p.m. until 11:15 p.m.?"

Rosalia had herself back in control now and replied, "That was the night Katherine died, and I remember being with my boyfriend."

"He'll confirm that he was in your home with you at that time?"

"No, I went to his apartment, but he'll confirm he was with me the entire evening. It was close to midnight when I got home."

"You understand that it is in your best interest if you give me his contact information."

Rosalia nodded and gave it to her. Embarrassed, she said, "Sorry for having lost my cool, but the memory of what happened years ago is upsetting." She got to her feet and said, "I need to head back to court."

They walked out the door together and, before they parted, Rosalia said, "Has it occurred to you that Katherine's death has nothing to do with what she mentioned at the book club meeting and that it was accidental and a pure coincidence?"

"I don't believe in coincidences," said Suzanne.

At home Suzanne got out her notebook and realized that she had not kept it current. So far, she had only added the following comments:

Violet: *Very weak motive concerning a rape case of 10 years ago. As to alibi, she claimed to have been at home alone.*

Charlotte: *No known motive, but the fact that she made that probing call to Katherine is indication that she has a dark secret. As to alibi, she claimed to have been at home. No doubt her husband will verify it. Can one trust a spouse's confirmation?*

Luke: *No known motive, but he clearly does not want me to investigate. As to alibi, he is another person who claims to have been home alone.*

Now she added:

Maxine: *I sensed hostility when I questioned her. Was her "Don't tempt fate! You will regret it if you do." a threat? Her alibi is a séance she held in her shop. She claims to have three persons to substantiate the fact.*

Rosalia: *On the surface her motive - - the thing about pushing the other girl accidentally into the street in front of a car - - is weak. On the other hand, she believes she committed a crime. As for alibi, she claims to have spent the crucial time at her boyfriend's.*

To be fair, Suzanne decided to add Brian to the suspect list.

Brian: *No known motive. He thinks that Katherine's death was accidental and that I'm wasting my time. His alibi is that he landed at LAX from his New York flight at 9:10 p.m. and that he drove himself home, arriving around 10:30. As for verification: I heard him come home but did not look at the time.*

The last one left to interview was Theo Oxley. She did not expect great success from a talk with him. Being a police officer, he would most likely know how to cover his tracks if he did have something to hide.

CHAPTER 21

Early Friday morning of that week, Theo Oxley was on his routine jog at Crescenta Valley Park. He had started at the dog park, made his way across the wash, and was now running on the slight downhill trail next to the embankment. He had encountered few people this early in the day; a couple walking their dog and a lone mountain bike rider was the extent of it so far. The crisp morning air with a temperature of 60 degrees Fahrenheit suited him fine for a run.

As a rule when out jogging, he concentrated on his breathing and tried to keep his mind free of pondering, but now he thought back to the phone conversation he'd had with Suzanne. He had told her he was too busy to see her, unless she was willing to meet him at Crescenta Valley Park between 7:00 and 7:30 a.m. To his surprise, she took him up on it and said that she wasn't due for work at the library until 9:00.

He slowed down his pace as he reached the end of the park and crossed back over the wash, where the terrain turned uphill. Next, he passed a kids' playground area with swings and slides to his right and a baseball field to his left. When he reached the steep hill leading up to the skateboard court, he changed his step to a walk.

There was not a soul performing skateboard or scooter tricks in the arena but Suzanne was already sitting in the bleachers, waiting for him.

He plopped himself down next to her and said, "I can tell that you're freezing. Let's get this over with fast."

She asked him where he was the night of Katherine Scherrer's death, which had become her routine.

He replied, "I was hanging out with some pals from the force at The Toast that night."

"In that case, you won't mind if I check with the bartender at the pub, and you give me your colleagues names?"

"I'll comply, with the understanding that you'll be discreet," and he mentioned two officers, whose names she entered into her iPhone.

Knowing that there was no chance that he would open up about anything in his past, she was about to end the interview when an idea popped into her head.

She said, "Being a layperson, I find it extremely hard to do background checks on the persons involved. I'm asking you for help in the matter."

"I'm not a detective," he stated.

"I know, but I'm sure with a little effort, you'll get access to criminal records."

"Whom do you have in mind?"

With a sheepish smile she replied, "I have some motive ideas for Violet and Rosalia, but I'd appreciate if you'd do a background check on the rest of the book club members."

"That's a tall order! Are you sure you want to go through with this investigation of yours?"

"A hundred percent."

"I'll see what I can do but am making no promises."

And this time it was he who cracked a smile when saying, "You can't possibly expect me to reveal any of my own dark secrets."

"Not unless you volunteer them," she replied.

CHAPTER 22

By Saturday evening, Suzanne realized that she was barely into the book they were to discuss at the March meeting, which was going to be held next Wednesday, March 9. Consequently, she forced herself to sit and read. The story was a memoir, a genre she liked, but these days she could not concentrate, catching her mind wandering to her self-appointed murder investigation.

Brian was only stationed at home base for another ten days and then he was flying out of New York again. She wished she could discuss what she silently called "her case" with him but that seemed out of the question. He was clearly against her pursuing the matter and seemed almost hostile whenever she brought up the subject.

It was frustrating how little progress she'd made so far, hoping that Theo would supply her with additional motives for murder where her suspects were concerned. In regards to alibis, she had checked out the ones that had been given to her. They had turned out as expected. Charlotte's husband verified that she was home during the crucial time on the night of the alleged murder. All of the three séance attendants confirmed Maxine's claim that she had been at her shop. Same with Rosalia's boyfriend, who swore she was at his apartment the entire time. As for Brian; he drove home from the airport and, although she had been only halfway awake, she'd heard him come home.

She had not had time yet to contact the two officers Theo had mentioned he'd shared drinks with at The Toast on the night in question, nor did she swing by that local pub to question the bartender, but she was positive they all would back up Theo's story.

Violet and Luke had no one to substantiate that they had been home alone. In other words, neither had an alibi. That in itself didn't mean anything. Suzanne had read enough mysteries to know that detectives in general were suspicious of airtight alibis.

She sighed and guided her attention back to the open book in her lap, being aware that she needed to read an additional 200 pages before Wednesday.

On Tuesday Suzanne received an e-mail message from Theo Oxley which read:

"I was able to uncover some dirt in a couple of our book club members' past, and I'm working on another. I'll give you my report when it is complete. Also, I'm waiting to give you the information until after tomorrow's meeting. I'm sure you want to avoid any awkwardness at our group gathering."

Suzanne thought, the meeting may turn out to be awkward even without Theo's contribution.

CHAPTER 23

The March book club meeting at Suzanne and Brian's house was getting under way. The members were careful not to mention Katherine Scherrer's name, nor anything that happened after their February meeting, even though the author was on everyone's mind. In other words, people desperately wanted the gathering to be a "book club business as usual" type thing. After they chose their refreshments and sat down at the large table, the thumbs-up or thumbs-down routine was taking place.

When it was Charlotte's turn to give the current book a thumbs approval or disapproval, followed by an explanation of the rating, she did no such thing. Instead, she stood up for emphasis and said, "I did not read the book. In fact, I'm quitting the club. I just came to give you a piece of my mind. I halfway expected to find some semblance of a memorial here today, or at least a minute of silence, if not a prayer. But no, you all act as if nothing had happened. Silently, though, the innocent among you are wondering who the killer is in our midst, and the person responsible for Katherine's death is trying to act as natural as possible."

The spunky redhead took a few seconds to inhale and then continued, "Other than reading one of her books and meeting her here last month, I did not know Katherine personally, but I went to her funeral. Lots of fans showed up to mourn her, but the saddest thing was seeing her family in deep grief, including her granddaughter, who can't be older than kindergarten age.

"At least whoever killed her was not hypocritical enough to attend. The one person of our group I saw from a distance was Suzanne, and she can't be the criminal, since she's doing the investigating. Or can she?"

Charlotte eyed Suzanne with suspicion and continued, "I kept your own secret until now, but can't hold my tongue any longer. You're pointing fingers at everybody else, but Katherine must have learned what really happened to your kid sister."

Suzanne just stared and the nurse ranted on, "I was doing my student nurse internship at the local hospital when they brought the girl's body in. When I first joined the book club, you looked familiar, but I didn't put two and two together until only the other day. You were in your teens and you cried over your little sister's death and kept saying it was all your fault."

She paused and then said in a matter-of-fact way, "And if anyone is in doubt about me, I'm in business to save lives, not take lives."

Maxine started to say something but Charlotte put up her hand and said, "Let me finish. I've enjoyed belonging to this group and hate to see it end, but I really don't have much time to read these days and now is the right moment for me to quit. You people have a good session if you can stomach it."

Having gotten that off her chest, she walked past them and out the door.

The only sound heard in the room for the next few seconds was the intake of Suzanne's breath. Then she pinched herself to make sure what had just happened was real. At the same instant Theo thought, either Charlotte is innocent of Katherine's murder, or she put on a convincing show.

Brian broke the silence and stated, "Contrary to what my better half is up to, I believe that the writer's drowning was nothing more than a tragic accident. The woman fell asleep while taking a bath and slid under water. End of story. I propose we go on with the business of discussing the current book."

Maxine chimed in, "I agree. We came to deliberate the memoir, so let's get to it."

Everyone followed Brian's suggestion but their hearts weren't in it. Debating the book suddenly seemed trivial, compared with what had happened in their real lives. The meeting broke up much earlier than expected.

Left by themselves and clearing away the dishes, Brian asked, "Why didn't you tell me that you attended the author's funeral?"

Suzanne replied, "Would you have approved?"

"No."

"There's your answer."

In bed that night Brian turned to her and whispered, "I hate that this Katherine thing is pulling us apart."

"Having sex won't make the problem go away," she replied.

CHAPTER 24

Another rendezvous took place at Crescenta Valley Park's skateboard court on Friday morning, March 11. This time there were a couple of scooter riders in the arena. Suzanne and Theo watched as they performed their tricks in the pit. The show was spectacular, even though the two teens paid no attention to their audience.

Observing one of the boys performing a double flip high into the air, Suzanne said, "I'm glad they're wearing helmets."

Theo remarked, "Either they're practicing for an upcoming competition, or they're here to get a good adrenaline rush. But let's get to the purpose of our meeting."

He reached for his phone and stated, "I wrote it down, even though I practically know it all by heart. Here goes:

"Maxine Dupont, aka Madame Maxine: She used to be Max Dupont, way back, but you may already have guessed something like that. As to her record; there was a case against her but it settled out of court. It seems that at one of her fortune telling sessions she predicted that it lay in the cards that her client would soon be free of her antagonist, and a few days later, that person ended up killing her husband she considered the antagonist. Her client claimed that Madame Maxine made her do it. As I said, the lawsuit settled out of court, so that's all I could conjure up."

Suzanne put in, "So even if there was no trial, if word got around about this, her psychic business would suffer."

Theo continued, "Luke Grey: His current record as financial advisor is spotless, but there exist some shady doings many years back when he worked as accountant for a major tech company."

"What kind of shady doings?" Suzanne wanted to know.

"Nothing was ever proven but there had been an investigation of embezzlement."

"I see."

"Like I said, there was no proof and the inquiry was dropped. He was not even fired but quit the job of his own accord. Still, my moto in these cases is always, *there's no smoke without fire.*"

Theo went on with his report, "Charlotte Chadwick: She does not have a criminal record. I happen to be friends with a male nurse who works with her at the same hospital. According to him, she is a strong advocate for assisted suicide. There is no evidence whatsoever that she ever acted on her conviction, though.

"Brian Morlett: I could not find any dirt on your husband. His slate is as unsoiled as Mr. Clean's detergent."

"I should hope so!"

He continued, "That takes care of all the info you asked for. I did not search for any records of Violet and Rosalia, since you told me that you did a background check on them yourself."

"I didn't have to," she said. "They more or less volunteered their information about a possible motive."

Theo said, "Since I'm at it, it's only fair that I wash my own dirty laundry. I have given the author's accusation some thought. The sole incident I can come up with that Katherine could have referred to concerning me occurred three years ago. At that time, a police brutality scrutiny involving me took place. I was being investigated for using excessive force during an arrest. I had chased the guy on my motorcycle for half an hour and my adrenaline was working overtime when I finally caught up with him, and I pummeled him with my fists. The criminal had to be hospitalized but fully recovered. The investigation had been held within the police force and I was found innocent of any wrongdoing. It taught me a lesson, though."

Suzanne said, "I appreciate your honesty."

One of the teens came leaping backwards, high into the air on his scooter near the bleachers, and for a split second it looked as if he'd fly straight at them. Suzanne suppressed a scream as the boy changed direction in mid-air and landed on a railing, parallel with the pit.

Theo laughed and remarked, "The kid scared you for a sec!" Then he got serious once again and said, "Do you want my personal opinion about this whole Katherine Scherrer business?"

"Yes, please."

"While listening to Katherine's rant at the February meeting, it first occurred to me that the woman was having her fun with us. She seemed to throw out her accusation, waiting to see who would take the bait, with the sole purpose to amuse herself. I also have enough life experience to know that if by chance her comments would hit home with someone in our group, she could be in for more than she'd bargained for. As you may remember, I even warned her that she was playing a dangerous game.

"After she was killed, I came to the conclusion that I had been wrong in my guess, and that her comment must have been aimed at one person who could ill afford being exposed. Like you, I did not buy the idea that her drowning was accidental. I reasoned that she most likely recognized that person with a criminal past, and he or she silenced Katherine before she got a chance to take it to the authorities."

Giving her a meaningful glance, he added, "But now it looks like five out of eight people are harboring a damaging secret. That seems a bit steep, but let's face it, the facts show that we belong to a *dark* book club."

He concluded with, "I've changed my mind again at this point and go with my original opinion that the author was throwing things out for her own amusement, and that she did not know anyone in the group prior to that meeting in February, nor was she aware of any crime committed. Sadly, her game backfired. One of our members took her seriously and thought she needed to be silenced."

Suzanne had listened to him carefully and then said, "The idea that Katherine meant it all as a joke never occurred to me, but you may be right. So the whole thing could have been avoided. I feel even stronger in my conviction that I'm partly to blame for her death, since I invited her in the first place and owe it to her to get justice."

He got up, ready to continue his jog, then turned to her and warned, "I understand what you're compelled to do, but be extremely careful. You may not play games like the writer did, but you're still putting yourself in danger.

Remember, you're dealing with a killer who didn't hesitate to silence Katherine and will not hesitate to silence you, if he or she feels threatened by what you're doing."

"Thanks for being concerned, but I'm well aware of all that and am on my guard," she said, and waved him good-bye.

She sighed and glanced toward the skateboard court and thought, I wish I could be as carefree as those daredevil boys. Then she also got up and walked to where her car was parked.

CHAPTER 25

After getting home from the library that day, Suzanne applied herself to some serious thinking. Not only did she rehash what Theo had said at CV Park in the morning but also what she had uncovered so far.

She had driven by Katherine's house when she first got the idea into her head that the lady may not have met with an accidental death. The author had lived in a fairly remote street in the Lake View Terrace area. As far as Suzanne knew, there had been no evidence of a break-in. So she came up with two scenarios. Either the culprit had been let in by Katherine herself, or had picked the lock.

What could have been a reason that the lady of the house would have invited the person in? she wondered. Granted, they were not complete strangers, but Katherine had met the individual on the night of the book club meeting for the first time, assuming that Theo's idea was correct. Namely, that Katherine's claim that she "never forgot a face, nor a voice" was pure bluff on her part and that she had faced a room full of strangers at that moment.

It was doubtful that the adept writer would have let a mere acquaintance into her house under the circumstances, especially not late in the evening. And she would certainly not take a bath while the person was still in her home. So the criminal must have picked the lock, she concluded.

But why wait a week before killing her if the person felt threatened by what Katherine had said at the meeting? That did not make sense. If the suspect thought she might go to the authorities with her information, the time to act would have been sooner rather than later.

Suzanne's phone rang. She let it go to voicemail as she was unwilling to interrupt her train of thought.

The ringing of it gave her an idea. "Of course!" she said aloud. "The phone call." According to Charlotte, several members of the club had phoned Katherine, curious whom the lady had targeted with her remark. The killer must have been making one of those calls. Was it possible that blackmail could be involved? Suzanne shook her head and thought, I can't picture Katherine as a blackmailer; that's absurd. What if the murderer assumed they were being blackmailed? I think that's it. By George, I think I've got it! She told herself.

So if Theo is correct with his assumption that Katherine was just playing with them and her claim meritless, the killer not only took her seriously but believed that she was blackmailing them. Charlotte had told her that Katherine knew who she was talking to during their phone conversation, even though Charlotte had tried to disguise her voice. So the villain probably did the same and was also recognized, or at least thought so.

Another bait e-mail is in order, Suzanne decided, and promptly composed one that she sent individually to all book club members, except Charlotte and Rosalia, as she already knew about their calls to Katherine. The e-mail read:

"I am finally getting somewhere with my investigation. I figured out who called Katherine that day before she was killed.

She recognized the person's voice even though it was disguised. 'There is such a thing as a clear speech pattern,' she told me.

"*Likewise, she said, it did not take a genius to know who the caller was, since she had recognized the person the minute introductions had been made at the book club meeting.*

"*I have something else up my sleeve, and if proven, that knowledge will incriminate you beyond any reasonable doubt.*

"*Katherine also hinted that running into that shady person by pure chance may be worth her while. I think she was talking blackmail. Am I right?*

"*Let me be clear: Blackmail on my part is the farthest from my mind. All I'm after is to solve the mystery of Katherine's death. I'm willing to listen to your side of what happened.*"

She signed off with,

"*Do the right thing and confess.*

"*Suzanne*"

She got a couple of reactions to her message but not the kind she had hoped for.

Theo called and said, "I see. You are continuing the dangerous game the author started. It is obvious to me that you sent a similar e-mail to other members too. I am not amused and neither is the killer, I would bet. You took the pain of sending your message individually instead of in a group e-mail, counting on the guilty person taking it as a direct accusation. I'd watch my back carefully, if I were you!"

Suzanne replied, "Don't worry. I'm on my guard. Brian is flying out of Burbank these days, so I'm not alone at night for long, and if I am, I'm taking precautions. There are always plenty of people around me at the library and the same goes for when I'm at the zoo on Mondays."

"I still don't like what you did. You're provoking the criminal to come forward. You can hardly be serious about a confession, like you wrote. What you hoped to accomplish is for the culprit to take the bait and come forward. But what you'll get is an infuriated perpetrator who will stop at nothing to silence you."

"I do appreciate your concern, but I've got this under control," she assured him.

Brian was furious with her that night and shouted, "What the heck is the matter with you? Accusing me of blackmail, among other things!"

"The blackmail, if indeed it was done, refers to Katherine having been the blackmailer. Read the e-mail carefully."

"I read it on my iPhone at the airport and then deleted it right away, too angry to look at it again. Are you out of your mind, accusing me of having anything to do with her death?"

She said, "Sorry, hon, but I couldn't leave anyone out of our group to be fair. Besides, this way I didn't have to explain to you what I wrote to the book club members. You could read it for yourself."

"It did not look like a group mail; it was only addressed to me. Are you saying that you sent it out to all members individually?"

"Yes, except for Charlotte and Rosalia. I had already discussed their phone calls to Katherine during the interviews I held with them."

He had calmed down when he realized her e-mail had been sent to all club members as a bait. Now his anger flared up again and he said, "So you made an exception for those two women but not for your husband!"

"As I mentioned, I'd like to keep the investigation impartial and professional."

"That's just it! You're not a professional but take it upon yourself to play detective. Accusing your husband of killing someone, no less. We've been married for over 19 years, and I thought I knew you. It turns out that I don't know you at all!"

He then stormed out of the room and slammed the door shut.

CHAPTER 26

The killer was convinced that silencing the writer had been a necessity and had done so without hesitation. Suzanne was an entirely different challenge and hard to deal with. Katherine had been a stranger. The current situation was personal and tough to carry out. Scruples aside, Suzanne also needed to be dealt with. As hard as that would be, self-preservation was at stake. There was no knowing what she had up her sleeve, nor when she would act on it.

The culprit had tried to come up with a gameplan but rejected each one as too risky. Another accidental death would be suspicious following this close to the first. And an undisputed homicide needed to be executed to perfection, pointing equally to any one of seven book club members.

There was not much time to come up with a full proof idea. Suzanne may inform the authorities at any moment, but would probably wait a few days - - being willing to listen - - like she wrote in her e-mail. In frustration, the person put the scheming aside for the moment and reached for the Los Angeles Times.

By pure chance, the perpetrator stumbled on an advertisement. The promotion read, *A Children's Day at the Zoo*. The date was Monday, March 14. Not only would there be free admissions for kids on that day, but special entertainment, including rides and characters dressed up as animals, throughout the park.

They're trying to copy Disneyland but no doubt can't compete, the individual thought.

About to turn the paper to the next page, the person was hit by a brainstorm. Suzanne volunteered at the zoo on Mondays, which was common knowledge among the book club members. March 14 was in two days! The culprit checked the work calendar for that day and nodded, thinking, it's doable, then studied the information about the Children's Day at the Zoo more closely, rereading it multiple times.

A plan of action was formed that same instant. With good timing and a bit of luck, it should work like a charm.

CHAPTER 27

The Children's Day at the Zoo was in full swing. After a couple days of gloom, the weather had turned back to sunshine and perfect spring temperatures of near 80 degrees. The place had filled with parents pushing their toddlers in strollers, kids of all ages, class excursions, and the general public. They all took advantage of the special attractions offered.

The people dressed up as zoo animals had long donned their costumes and been given instructions to mingle throughout the park. The culprit picked a particularly animated creature in a black bear outfit to follow around, figuring that sooner or later there would be an opportunity to strike.

Sure enough, the droll bear character vanished into an all-gender restroom and his pursuer followed. When the dressed-up bear entered a large handicap stall and turned around to close the door, his shadow had already done so, saying, "Let me help you with this," and pulled the head portion of the bear's costume off. The unfortunate individual did not see the chloroform held under his nose coming and went out like a light.

A couple of minutes later, a freshly clad black bear came out of the handicap stall and placed an "out of order" sign at its door. On the way out, the bear waved to kids and their parents entering the restroom. Working the grounds from exhibit to exhibit, the new bear quickly adjusted to the role of entertaining children of all ages, by beckoning to the young ones and flirting with the teens, while constantly keeping an eye out for his prey.

The docents were easy to spot with their red polo shirts, lecturing to a bunch of kids. There had been one near the crocodile lair and another by the gorillas. An hour had passed since the bear character's quest began and, so far, there was no sight of Suzanne. It was getting hot and uncomfortable under the animal costume, but the perpetrator put mind over matter and continued the search. Now it made sense why the original bear character had only worn underwear beneath the costume.

The criminal came around to the Asia zone - - and there she was, standing with her back inches away from the fence of the Sumatran tiger exhibit, talking to a group of kids about the natural habitat of the species. The villain took in the scene of fence, moat, and tigers beyond the moat and thought, this is perfect! Given a choice, I could not have picked a better spot for my purpose.

The bear character waited until the end of Suzanne's speech and then approached the group, waving, shaking the youngsters' hands, humming a tune, and advancing toward the docent with inviting dance steps. Getting close to her, the make-believe bear extended a hand. Suzanne took him up on it and they did a bit of jitterbug dancing - - to amuse her audience, she thought.

Without warning, and by sheer force of adrenaline, the person in the bear disguise flung her over the fence and hurled her so hard that she cleared the water-filled moat. She would have landed smack in the tiger exhibit, had it not been for a large tree she hit her head on and then held on to one of its branches for dear life.

There were frightened screams as everyone focused on the docent. Nobody paid attention to the bear figure, who quietly slipped away while reasoning, there's no way she can hold on to that branch for long. If the tigers don't get her, she'll suffer fatal injuries from the fall.

After finding a quiet spot, the person shed the animal costume and then leisurely walked among the crowds toward the zoo's exit.

As for Suzanne, she was blinded by the stream of blood flowing from her head wound. She closed her eyes, still holding on to the tree branch, knowing that she could not last much longer. About to lose her grip, she heard sirens, and seconds later she felt a harness around her waist and a firefighter saying, "You can let go; I've got you now."

While being transported to the nearest hospital, Suzanne was barely conscious, but thought, I'm dealing with a killer who is more dangerous and resourceful than expected.

When the group of kids and other bystanders were questioned; nobody could identify the attempted murderer. After all, it had just been a friendly dancing bear. Likewise, the original wearer of the bear costume, found in undergarments after regaining consciousness, could not identify the culprit either.

That witness stated, "I only got a glimpse of the person, who wore a facemask, before I was oblivious to the world." When asked about the attacker's gender, the answer was, "I don't know; it all happened in a split second."

CHAPTER 28

Suzanne "was resting comfortably" in her hospital bed. At least, that was the phrase the medical staff used. If one had asked Suzanne herself, she was anything but comfortable. The concussion had given her an enormous headache, and the extensive head wound was throbbing. The cuts and bruises on her arm and leg were superficial lacerations but added to her discomfort.

A nurse flitted in, taking her vital signs, and on her way out said, "You have a visitor."

Brian bent down to kiss his wife gently on the cheek. She looked extremely vulnerable, with her partly shaved scalp and sutures showing through clear adhesive tape that ran from the top of her head down to her temple.

Tearing up, he said, "Thank God you're going to be okay. I talked with the doctor. He sounded reassuring. They'll take a CAT scan to make sure that there is no brain damage."

Suzanne asked, "What time is it?"

"Ten past three."

"What about your flight to Seattle?"

He smiled and replied, "I can see that your brain still works! The 1:00 p.m. flight to Seattle was cancelled because of bad weather up there. I was on stand-by when notified about the assault on you. They found someone to take my place for the re-routing."

He touched her hand lightly and said, "You are lucky to be alive. Promise me you'll stop your so-called investigation. Your attacker may well try again. I'll be based in New York starting Saturday and can't watch out for you."

Instead of a promise she replied, "It took an attempt at my life for you to realize that I was correct about Katherine."

"So true. I'm sorry." And after a pause he said, "But promise?"

She closed her eyes and mumbled, "I have a tremendous headache and need to sleep now."

Sleep was not an option, she realized, as they rolled her out for the CAT scan.

Hours later, although exhausted, Suzanne still had not fallen into a deep sleep. She had dozed a bit, but the wheels inside her sore head kept turning. The CAT scan had shown no evidence of brain damage, making both Brian and her sigh with relief. The doctors wanted to keep her at the hospital for observation for a day or two, but her outlook was good.

She was about to relax when two police officers showed up and conducted a brief questioning, hoping she'd be able to identify her attacker. One was in plain clothing, the other in uniform. She shook her head, which shot waves of pain up and down her skull. The nurse had warned her about keeping her head still. When they asked if she had enemies, or whether she could shed light on the reason for the assault, she answered in the negative. At this point, she did not find it necessary to enlighten the authorities about her theory of Katherine's death. It would be better to wait until she had some concrete information to give them.

They pressured her again with things like, "You must have at least an idea of why you were attacked." And, "If you won't tell us who has a grudge against you, we are in a difficult position to launch an investigation."

When she assured them once more that she had no idea who the culprit was, and that she did not have any enemies, the lead officer stated, "We'll treat it as a random attack for now, until more information comes to light."

To her relief, her attending physician stepped into the room at that moment and told them she needed to rest, which ended their questioning.

In the evening, she sent Brian home to get some rest, while she intended to sleep at long last. But instead, she mulled over the possible identity of her assailant.

She could eliminate Violet and Rosalia. Both women were too short and could not have had the strength to hurl her over the fence. Even allowing for the bear costume to add an inch or two to the person's height, the culprit was at least as tall as herself but most likely taller. Considering the power needed, the male members of the book club and Maxine and Charlotte would qualify. Maxine was big and muscular, and the nurse would have had plenty of practice lifting patients in and out of their beds.

As to opportunity, any one of them using a bit of imagination could have swiped the black bear getup as a disguise. All club members knew about her volunteer work at the zoo on Mondays. She had had no suspicion that anyone other than the person hired by the zoo administration had been dressed up as the animal character, and so she had played along with the little charade of a happy dance. The person had counted on that.

There was nothing in the "bear's" demeanor that would give the person away. The individual's gait had been a bit awkward, which was only natural under the heavy costume. The dancing, on the other hand, had been well performed, but she had no idea who among the book club members would be good dancers. And heck, the beast had not uttered a single word, so there was no chance of a voice recognition.

Frustrated, she thought, I'm going at this the wrong way. I need to backtrack and reflect on what I've learned during the interviews. But at that moment her injured body took over and she fell into a restless slumber.

CHAPTER 29

When releasing Suzanne from the hospital on Thursday, the attending doctor mentioned that she would experience headaches for several weeks and forbade her strenuous activities and sudden jerky movements. He stressed that lots of rest would help with her recovery. Consequently, she was on sick leave from the library until further notice.

Her near-miss fatality had been broadcast over the news and social media. During the next few days, co-workers as well as friends and relatives relayed their concerns by phone, e-mail, or text, and some even sent flowers with messages of good wishes.

Brian showered her with tender loving care, the likes of which had been missing during the last few weeks. Even Warren pulled out of his teenage self-centeredness and showed deep concern for her wellbeing. To her and Brian's astonishment, he did the cooking that first evening his mom came home from the hospital.

Violet made the following emotional call:

"I'm so glad to hear your voice, and thank God you're alive! How are you feeling?"

"I've got a headache but I'm on the mend."

"I wish you'd taken my advice and left the whole thing alone."

Suzanne replied, "You know that I felt I owed it to Katherine. Part of me still does but part of me is afraid now."

"As well you should be. Tell me the truth, how are you really?"

"The assault was a jolt to my system, both physically and emotionally, but like I said, I'm recovering."

"I hope you have learned your lesson and will leave the detecting to the authorities now."

Suzanne cut her short and answered, "I'm getting tired. Hope you don't mind if we hang up," and ended the call.

One by one, the rest of the book club members contacted her with similar wishes and concerns.

All this attention was more of a burden to Suzanne than a comfort, and she voiced it to Brian with an attempt at humor, saying, "Our place looks like a funeral parlor with all those flowers and people's good wishes."

"Make sure this is not a rehearsal for the real thing coming," he replied, trying to sound lighthearted, but she knew that deep down he was serious. She wished that she could reassure him that she'd drop her investigation, but could not bring herself to do or say so. Right now, all she wanted was to rest and feel healthy again, but she knew herself well enough to be certain that once her body was back to normal, the urge to solve the mystery of Katherine's death would be greater than the fear of the aggressor.

Like all others, her attacker voiced concern for her, seemingly full of compassion, but thought, too bad it did not go according to plan. There is no way I could have foreseen that she'd hit the tree branch and hold on to it. For her own good, I'm keeping my fingers crossed that the episode at the tiger exhibit scared her enough to stop her from snooping. And if not, the next attack will be hitting its mark, I'll make sure of that.

CHAPTER 30

The brutal attack on Suzanne put the book club members in a pensive mood. Even the ones who had clung to the idea that Katherine's death had been accidental were now forced to change their minds. They refrained from mentioning their suspicions out loud, but secretly mulled over who they suspected of being the villain.

Brian thought that Theo would be the most likely person. As police officer, he would know how investigations were handled and would easily avoid falling into any traps the investigating detective would lay. Picking a lock would be easy as pie for him. The man would also have more than enough strength to hurl Suzanne over the moat at the zoo.

Theo, for his part, tagged Charlotte as the culprit. The woman had a forceful personality and was not afraid of anyone. If someone crossed her, she would not hesitate to act. She must have thought that Katherine knew a ruinous secret of hers and felt that her self-preservation was at stake. She is also a cool-headed actress. That performance she gave at the March club meeting, accusing the rest of us of being heartless and doing "business as usual" was extremely effective.

Violet picked Luke as the killer. As guest at that book club meeting, Katherine had faced him directly at the opposite end of the long table. And when the author made her accusing remarks, she had seemed to look straight at him. The man gives the appearance of such a respectable citizen, but she guessed that was only show. In fact, she had never really liked him.

Maxine chuckled to herself and mused that most of the book club members were capable of murder if provoked, including herself. If she were asked to pinpoint the deed to someone in particular, she'd pick Brian. That fellow had a shifty eye.

Luke had a similar idea, thinking that Suzanne may suspect any of them. She may know incriminating secrets some of the group's members may be desperate to protect. As for the attack on her, she may well rule out Violet and maybe Rosalia. She would doubt that either one would have been strong enough to send the librarian flying, even during an adrenaline rush.

And finally, there was Charlotte, who tagged Maxine as being the criminal. She did not trust the psychic. She had always felt that the woman was a phony and that she used the Madame Maxine business to further her own agenda. Who knew what shady deals she had gotten away with under the guise of predicting the future.

Rosalia was the only person out of the group that did not dwell on the subject at hand. Her boyfriend had recently proposed marriage, and the young woman was on cloud nine, preoccupied with planning her wedding and a bright future.

CHAPTER 31

Early Saturday morning, March 19, Brian left for JFK, where he was scheduled to be stationed for a month. Before leaving, he tiptoed into the dim master bedroom where Suzanne lay in a semi slumber.

He bent over her, kissed her on the forehead, and whispered, "I'll call you from New York."

She mumbled, "Okay."

"And please be careful. Promise me, no more sleuthing!"

She did not answer, having already drifted off again.

Hours later, Suzanne got out of bed and tried to start her day as normal as possible. Her head still hurt, but she decided to skip the painkiller medication, forcing her body to heal itself and get back to normal.

She fixed some breakfast - - or lunch, according to the time of day - - when Warren entered the kitchen and said, "Are you okay if I go to the park and kick the ball around with my friends?"

"Why wouldn't I be? Did Dad put you up to babysitting me?"

Embarrassed, her son replied, "He said to watch over you, but I'm worried and want to do so on my own."

"Thanks for being concerned, but you needn't be. I'm recovering well from the concussion, and as for your other worry, I'm not going to do anything that could put me in danger. So go have fun!"

Left by herself, Suzanne enjoyed her brunch and then decided to tidy up the master bedroom. As per doctor's orders, she was to abstain from housework for at least a couple of weeks, but she didn't consider making the bed entailed any hard work.

Straightening up, she noticed a toiletry bag Brian had accidentally left behind on the dresser. She checked the time. Too late to reach him on his cellphone - - making calls was not allowed when in flight. She shrugged to herself and reasoned, there's nothing I can do about it. Once he gets to the Airbnb and realizes he left the bag behind, he'll just have to purchase new toiletries.

She had already stepped out of the bedroom when she reconsidered. Maybe I'd better check to make sure he's not without his thyroid medication, and turned around.

No pills were in Brian's case. There was only a brush and comb, toothpaste and toothbrush, tiny scissors, a nailfile, and a wallet. Oh no! He left his wallet behind, she mused. But wait, his wallet is black, so what's this brown one doing in his bag?

She opened it and the first thing she saw was a New York driver license. What? This is someone else's wallet! Then she looked at the photo. No mistaking, it was Brian, except the name written on the license was *Bill Moran.*

Suzanne suddenly got dizzy and sat down on the edge of their bed. Don't panic, she told herself, there has to be an explanation.

After a couple minutes she found the emotional strength to look through the rest of the billfold. There was a medical insurance card, a credit card, and an athletics club membership, all made out in the name of Bill Moran. And tucked behind several bills of cash, there was a list of names with New York area code phone numbers. The last number did not correspond to a name, it just read "landline."

Brian is leading a double life; that's the explanation! She started to shake uncontrollably and her headache was back full force. Half an hour later, she had herself in control and could think rationally. There were two reasons she could come up with that made sense. The first would be that he led a life of crime on the East Coast and that of a law-abiding citizen on the West. The other, which was far more likely, would be that a woman was involved.

Then she applied logic and deduced that if he only carried on an affair, there would be no need for double identities. No, he must also be married to someone else, who'd be as clueless as she'd been. Most likely, this meant deceit for years. One does not create a second identity overnight.

Suzanne's heart suddenly turned to ice, and she twirled the piece of paper with the list of phone numbers in her fingers and decided to get to the bottom of it all, before Warren came back. She dialed the number listed under "landline."

A female voice answered and Suzanne asked, "Is this the Moran residence?"

"Sure."

"Are you Mrs. Moran?"

"Yes, and you are?"

"You don't know me but..."

"Save your speech, we're not interested."

"Please don't hang up," Suzanne pleaded, "I'm not a telemarketer nor a scammer, but I have information that concerns both of us."

"I'll give you two minutes," Lillian replied.

"Fair enough, but please sit down. My news is shocking."

Half an hour later, the two women ended the call and both their lives changed dramatically from that point forward.

On that night, unable to fall asleep, Suzanne remembered Brian's words at a recent confrontation: *I thought I knew you. It turns out that I don't know you at all.* Well, you SOB, it so happens that *I'm* the one who does not know *you* at all. What else have you been up to besides polygamy? she wondered.

CHAPTER 32

Brian had a demanding job in the cockpit due to bad weather. There was a major storm along the New England Coast, reaching all the way down to New York. Flights in and out of regional airports were delayed and when he, at long last, got permission to land, the final descent and the landing had been choppy, demanding all his concentration. In the passenger cabins - - regardless whether they were sitting in first class, business, or economy - - folks were vomiting right and left.

Rain came down like rapids at the airport as he waited in line at the taxi stand. Once in the cab and on the way to Lillian's apartment, he closed his eyes and relaxed, thankful that his cabbie was not the kind who liked to chat. It was good getting away from L. A. for a while and he would try not to worry about Suzanne. He opened his carry-on luggage and was about to switch wallets, when he discovered that the toiletry bag was missing.

"Stay calm," he told himself. Seconds later, he frantically backtracked his movements of that morning in his mind's eye. He had showered, shaved, brushed his teeth and ran a comb through his hair, and then added those items to the bag which already contained the New York wallet. He remembered coming out of the bathroom, toiletry bag in hand, when Warren stopped him in the hallway, pen and paper at the ready, asking him to sign a field trip slip to a local museum. Needing his hands free, he quickly reached through the master bedroom open door and placed the small bag on the dresser.

Crap, he thought, when going back to the bedroom later to kiss Suzanne goodbye, I must have forgotten to toss it into the carry-on! I've never been that careless before but having lots on my mind, I was distracted.

No need to panic, he assured himself. Suzanne is a trusting soul. When she finds the bag, she may glance inside, see the toiletries packed at the top and say to herself, "He'll just have to replace them in New York."

Then he thought, wait, that was the old Suzanne. But ever since she got it into her head to play the detective, she'd been full of mistrust.

As far as his stay in New York was concerned, he would have to wing it without his East Coast credentials. That was not a big problem, but he would need to be careful when Lillian was close by. Even that was not crucial. Why would she have any reason to look closely at his credit card, for instance? The only real issue would be any contact with the law, but he'd make sure that would not happen.

Not wanting to do it in the taxi, he decided to call Suzanne first chance he got and tell her not to worry about the bag and to set it aside for him. He checked the time; almost 10 o'clock at night at his end, seven in Los Angeles. He'd find a moment in the next two hours to make that call.

CHAPTER 33

Immediately after ending Suzanne's call, Lillian started pacing down the hallway of her apartment as far as the master bedroom and back to the entrance hall. She marched back and forth like a caged animal, muttering to herself, what a fool I've been! There were signs here and there over the years, but I ignored them all, wanting the best for us as a family.

She dropped the phone she was still holding, then kicked it out of her way, as she continued to pace. On occasion, she had wondered whether he might have affairs while stationed in the West, then shrugged it off, attributing the idea to her imagination. Well, this was way worse than affairs; it was a disaster. Bill was juggling another wife and family. Not only was he messing with a lot of people's lives, but bigamy is a crime.

She stamped her foot and said aloud, "You bastard!" Then she thought, I know what I have to do, even if it's going to brake Ali's heart.

By the time she needed to pick her little girl up from the dance studio, she had dried her tears, put cold compresses on her eyes, applied tons of makeup, and had herself somewhat in control.

On the subway ride home, Ali was an excited chatterbox, saying, "Oh Mommy, the dance recital is gonna be soooo much fun! I'm gonna be in two numbers: tap and hip hop. Miss Kelly said we have the tap routine down pat but the hip hop needs a little more work. We have one more class and then the rehearsal before showtime. I can hardly wait! Daddy is gonna be so proud of me! You did buy four tickets, for you and Daddy, plus two more for my friend Lacey and her mom, right?"

Lillian did not have the heart to tell her that Daddy was not going to attend. This was neither the place nor the time to have that conversation. She answered truthfully, "Yes, I bought four tickets, my little chatterbox."

CHAPTER 34

Turning the key in the lock to the apartment and reaching for the light switch, Brian announced, "Honey, I'm home!"

Lillian had been waiting for him in the dark, sitting in an upright chair in the entrance hall.

"Hello, Mr. Brian Morlett!" Her voice came back like a slap in the face. "You can turn around and go back where you came from. You're no longer welcome here."

"I can explain," he stammered.

"There's nothing to explain. I know it all. Had a nice chat with your other wife."

"It looks bad, but..."

"It doesn't just look bad, it *is* bad!"

She inhaled, and then let lose a torrent of accusations. "You double crossing charlatan! When we first met and I questioned your wedding band, you had the insolence to tell me that you were a widower and did not have the heart to take it off. I fell for it, thinking that it was sweet of you to honor your departed loved one.

"You pressed for a small wedding, suggesting that only my side of family and friends should attend. Your so-called reason was because both your parents were dead, you had no siblings, and you didn't mind not inviting any of your friends, so that there would be more room for mine. At the time I thought it was a generous gesture. Now I know it was all lies.

"And as far as those friends were concerned, you never talked about any of them, let alone made plans to get together, in eight years. I thought that was strange, but shrugged it off, assuming socializing with people you and your departed wife used to hang out with together would be too painful for you."

"I'm so sorry and ..."

She held up her hand and snapped, "I'm not finished. You'd better hear me out since this is our last conversation. There was your insistence that I could not call you but always had to wait for you to call. Your explanation was your job as a pilot. How naive of me. And then there was the time I suggested we could all fly to L. A. when you needed to be stationed there, and I could do some sightseeing with Ali while you worked. I don't remember what argument you had against my idea, but you wriggled yourself out of the deal."

She came up for air and he asked, "What did you tell Ali?"

"I haven't had the guts to break her heart yet. Maybe I'll do it tomorrow."

"I'd like to attend her recital."

"You've got some nerve!" she shouted. "As far as I'm concerned, we are not married and Ali is my sole responsibility. Thank God she is fast asleep and doesn't have to witness this disgusting scene."

And she stretched out her hand and said, "Hand me your key."

"Be reasonable."

She did not alter her stance until he took it off his keychain and handed it to her. She then pointed to the door and ordered, "I want you to leave now. You can text me an address and I'll have your belongings shipped to you. I want you out now!"

"It's ten o'clock. May I at least spend the night? I'll sleep on the sofa."

"Out!" she yelled, while getting up from her chair and pointing at the door once more.

Brian Morlett, aka Bill Moran, had no choice. He gathered his luggage, like a robot, and retreated. His emotional numbness continued on the elevator ride down to the lobby. Once there, he heard the rain in a relentless stream pelting down onto the sidewalk. He shook himself, like a dog getting out of water, then tried to think clearly about what to do.

Automatically, he reached for his phone, then caught himself before pushing the speed-dial. No point in calling Suzanne any longer. The cat was out of the bag, big time. Instead, he searched the web for a hotel vacancy this late at night.

CHAPTER 35

On Friday, April 1, nearly two weeks had passed since Suzanne's appalling discovery, and she tried to keep her emotions under control. After the initial shock, she had gone from hurt, bitterness, and anger, to realism. Physically, she was on the mend, getting stronger with each new day, and she was working hard on keeping her emotions in check. Breaking down at the library, where she planned to go back to work on Monday, would not do.

To her astonishment, Warren had taken the news about his father's double life in his stride. His initial reaction was an outburst of, "What a jerk!" But overall, he seemed calm. He had given her a spontaneous hug - - a rarity since becoming a teenager. She opted to wait to tell her older son the disturbing news; let him enjoy his carefree college life a bit longer. She also refrained from mentioning it to any of her friends and relatives. It was too painful a subject for her to discuss at this time.

As to her own frame of mind, regardless of the pain Brian's betrayal caused her, was he also capable of murder? she asked herself. A couple of weeks ago, she would have answered in the negative but was no longer sure. If he thought Katherine knew his secret and imagined that she was about to go to the authorities with her knowledge, he had a lot to lose. She mused, after 19 years of marriage I thought that I knew my husband inside out. It turns out that I didn't know him at all.

She shook her head. But the attack on me at the zoo? Was he capable of that? It seemed impossible, but then again, her husband was not the person she had thought him to be.

Step by step, Suzanne played the zoo episode back in her mind, from the moment the "black bear" showed up, waving to the kids and shaking their hands on his way over to her. She remembered clearly how he extended his "paw" in a gesture to invite her to dance, her acceptance, then a fast jitterbug dance, ending with the animal persona hurling her over the fence into the Sumatran tiger exhibit.

Could that have been Brian in the bear costume? she mused. Hard to believe, but then, nothing felt real to her any longer. If so, she was at least out of danger while he was stationed in New York.

That night, in order to keep her mind from dwelling on her problem, she watched a detective TV program. And bingo, the show gave her an idea. It would mean taking someone into her confidence, but she needed to take that risk in order to find out for sure whether or not Brian was the killer.

CHAPTER 36

The following morning Suzanne called Theo Oxley and was lucky the police officer was off duty on that Saturday.

"Are you feeling better?" he asked.

"Much better. I think I'm over the concussion and the rest of me is healing too."

"I hope you've given up your quest?"

"Not exactly. That's why I'm calling. I need your help," she replied.

"I'm not sure I'll like what you have in mind, but shoot."

"As you know, there's a police investigation pending about what happened at the zoo. The authorities are treating the attack on me as a random act of violence and are under the impression that the assailant doesn't know me."

"I wonder why?" he replied.

She heard the sarcasm in his voice and ignored the question and continued, "Can you find out if the black bear costume in question is being kept in police possession as evidence, and if so, have they done a DNA test on it?"

"That's a tall order. Do you have anyone's DNA in mind?"

"I do, and I can obtain it, but don't want to go through the trouble if the animal costume is no longer available to the police. Also, for now, I'd rather keep whose DNA I have in mind to myself."

Theo stated, "I don't want to know, but I'm sure you're not surprised that I'm interested in the assault case on you. I made a point to know who the investigating detective is."

"I hope you didn't mention to that detective that the attack on me is connected to Katherine's death. As you've already gathered, I'd like to wait with making it official until I have some evidence."

"Don't worry. I'll leave that up to you. In fact, I did not even mention the book club. I only told him that I knew you and was concerned. On the other hand, I did arrange for a patrol car to cruise around your place, now and then."

"Why?"

"As I said, I'm concerned."

"That arrangement doesn't sit well with me. It may make my neighbors uneasy."

"They'll get used to it."

After a pause Suzanne asked, "So you'll find out about the bear costume?"

"I'll try but can't make any promises," he said.

CHAPTER 37

Brian was assigned to fly New York to Dallas shifts and had done so for the past two weeks. He had Saturday, April 2 off and was not looking forward to it. Too much time to brood, he thought. Dispirited, he entered an Airbnb in Queens after a long Uber ride from JFK. To call his situation depressing was an understatement. He used to have two nice homes with two loving families; now he had none. His temporary digs, minimally furnished, were cheerless, and yes, lonely.

He had made numerous calls to Suzanne, but she never picked up. Maybe sometime in the future he'd be able to patch things up with her, but at present that was unfeasible. He had had his punishment coming and realized that now. Besides the emotional agony, knowing that he was a shunned man, the practical side of it was tearing at him as well. He was basically homeless at the moment, trying to replace stuff he'd kept in both households.

In a way it was a relief to only use his real name again. His Bill Moran persona was tucked away in a toiletry bag on the dresser of his former home in California. No doubt, as far as the airline he worked for was concerned, they had always solely known him as Brian Morlett. At least that fact was reassuring.

As he sat down to a lonely dinner - - a frozen pre-cooked meal he'd warmed up in the microwave - - his thoughts strayed to his kids. It was clear that Lillian wouldn't allow him contact with Ali. He couldn't even fight her for visitation rights. Strictly speaking, they were never legally married, and she had all the authority over their daughter. He missed his little Ali already, and for her part, he knew the poor girl would have a hard time being estranged from her daddy. As for his boys, they were old enough to decide whether or not to stay connected to him.

His thoughts dwelled on Suzanne once more. After her discovery of his double existence, was it possible that she also suspected him of being Katherine's killer? He found that hard to believe. And he was certain that she did not think he was capable of the attempted murder on her.

By the time he had swallowed the last bite of the tasteless meal, his mind was made up. He'd give it a rest for now. By the end of the month, when scheduled to fly out of LAX again, he'd work his way back into her life.

CHAPTER 38

Ten days later, on April 13, as Suzanne started to doubt that she would ever hear from Theo Oxley again, she received the following e-mail message:

"The appropriate department of our police force has the bear costume in question in their possession for evidence. They did indeed test the item for DNA and could not match it to any person listed in their database.

"If you want to proceed, the person in charge of the assault case on you is Lt. Sharp.

"Best,

"Theo"

Suzanne was ready. She had had plenty of time to figure out what to do. Even though her house was full of Brian's DNA, the question was how to obtain it and then transport it. She had thought of his pillow, a shoe, or a straw-hat he wore to the beach, but had no idea if these items would be easy to contaminate while handling and carrying. In the end, she thought of a simple solution. The toiletry bag he'd left behind was perfect. There would be plenty of his DNA in there. She had not touched anything but the wallet, and she'd remove that anyhow, as she did not want the police to know about the wallet and the information it contained.

Early the following morning, before work, Suzanne dropped in at the appropriate police station and asked to see Lt. Sharp. She was told to wait and someone went to check whether he was available. Minutes later, she was ushered into the lieutenant's office.

He had his own small space, set apart from the main large office at the station. The room was strictly functional, with a desk, computer and large monitor, a printer, a file cabinet, and several devices foreign to Suzanne. There were no personal memorabilia, like family photos or keepsakes.

The instant she saw his face, she recognized him as the leading police officer who had questioned her in the hospital. She remembered that he had introduced himself and his assistant at the time, but that she had been too traumatized by her situation to pay attention to names.

He did not get up from behind his desk but motioned her to a chair in front of it, saying, "Hello, Mrs. Morlett, have a seat." As she did so, he continued, "So you thought about it and can give us an idea who your attacker might be?"

"Sort of," she replied. "I don't want to name the person just yet, in case I'm wrong, but I have DNA samples that you may be able to match to the DNA on the bear costume." She rummaged in her large purse, pulled out Brian's toiletry bag and, handing it to the lieutenant, added, "There is a brush and comb, a toothbrush, and some other minor items in there, belonging to the suspect I have in mind."

His glance was intent as he asked, "You did not obtain the items illegally?"

"No, sir."

"You're sure?"

"Yes, sir. The person accidentally left them with me."

He did not open the toiletry case, but grabbed an evidence bag from his desk drawer and dropped the case inside.

"Okay," he stated, "I'll send this to the lab. If it is a match, you are obligated to disclose the owner of the items to us. Understood?"

"Yes, sir. How long until you'll know?"

"I can't say. Depends on how backlogged the lab is. We have your phone number on file. I'll keep in touch."

With that, Suzanne felt herself dismissed.

CHAPTER 39

Lt. Sharp called Suzanne a few days later with the result. He said, "Sorry, Mrs. Morlett. The DNA samples taken from the costume and the ones from the articles you gave me are not a match."

"Thanks for letting me know," Suzanne managed to reply.

"If you have any other ideas or DNA samples handy, let me know," he added, not without sarcasm.

It was clear that Lt. Sharp was aware that she was not telling all she knew.

After hanging up, Suzanne was unsure how she felt. On the one hand, knowing that Brian had not been the killer was a relief; on the other, she had to start the investigation from scratch. Well, not exactly from scratch, but it did send her back to the drawing board.

That evening, while fixing spaghetti and meatballs for Warren and herself, Madame Maxine's tarot card reading popped into her head. Maxine had interpreted one of the cards with, "*You may accomplish what you seek but not without sacrifice.*" And another with, "*I see an unexpected change of course.*" Yet another she had construed as, "*Against all odds, you may accomplish your task.*" The sacrifice was her finding out about Brian's double life. The unexpected change of course would be Brian's innocence of the murder, and finally, Madame Maxine predicted that her investigation would be a success.

That was probably all rubbish, Suzanne thought. She did not believe that there was any truth in tarot card readings. Still, it was haunting that the psychic had been able to get so close to reality. Let's hope that her prophesy about my being successful also becomes true, she mused. And she tried hard not to think about the last card, the *Wheel of Fortune,* where Maxine warned, *"You are at the mercy of fate, don't tempt it!"* Again, she wondered if that last piece of advice was a warning or a threat.

Her thoughts reverted back to Brian. He was not a murderer, she mused, but that didn't absolve him from being a selfish, double-crossing SOB. She'd tell him so next time he made his ridiculous attempt at calling her.

At that point Warren walked into the kitchen, asking, "What's for dinner?" which pulled her out of her reverie.

CHAPTER 40

Suzanne had cancelled the April book club meeting, claiming that she was still recovering from her concussion and did not feel up to it. Her condition was a welcome excuse. The truth of the matter was that she could not face the group. The second Wednesday of the month fell on April 13. At that time she had trouble coping with the news she'd learned about Brian, and she also suspected him of being the killer. The idea that some club member would inquire how Brian was doing gave her the shivers.

As for the rest of the members, they also welcomed the postponement of the book club meeting. None had been willing to gather with a murderer in their midst. For some time now, they all believed that Katherine's death was no accident. They had gone as far as guessing who the killer might be, but at present, most made a point of putting the sordid subject out of their minds and went on with their lives.

The guilty person spent hours reflecting on what to do next. For right now, Suzanne seemed to put all energy into her recovery and on getting back to normal. Chances were great that, after the near miss attempt on her life, she was too frightened to continue her amateur detecting. At last, she must have become reasonable and grasped that her quest would bring her nothing but grief and wouldn't bring Katherine back.

The culprit re-read her latest e-mail message numeral times and came to the conclusion that the woman had been bluffing. Why would the author have confided in Suzanne and tell her who made that damaging phone call to her? Katherine was a stranger to Suzanne, like the writer had been to everyone else in the group. And the bit about knowing that blackmail was involved. Pure fabrication on Suzanne's part! She also had no idea who had been underneath the bear costume, the guilty person was positive about that. If the interfering woman would have a leg to stand on, she'd have gone to the police.

And finally, the perpetrator thought, this is all theory. I need to come up with another plan of silencing Suzanne, in case she continues her snooping at some point in the future. The important thing is to plot a foolproof way to do it. I can't afford to screw up again. There is no hurry this time around; I expect she'll contact me once more, if indeed she'll continue her amateurish investigation.

CHAPTER 41

Suzanne sat in front of the library computer, tending to the tedious job of checking inventory and deciding which books to order. She was more than qualified and competent to do so, but on Wednesday, April 20, she had a hard time concentrating. Instead, she would stare into space and think about her investigation.

She had checked her notes numerous times in the last few days and realized that she had been sloppy with taking them down, failing to write dialogue as she interviewed each person. In other words, she had only made general observations and comments. And pertaining to some conversations, she had nothing in writing at all.

In her mind's eye, she now rehashed every interview she'd had with each person, picturing their demeanor and trying to recall their exact words as she questioned them. She was thorough, going over every question she had asked and attempting to remember the answer, exactly in the wording it had been given. When finished, her head was throbbing, but she was none the wiser. Frustrated, she knew she was missing something important but was clueless.

Giving up, her eyes focused back on the computer screen, and she concentrated solely on her work for the remainder of the day.

Hours later, on her short drive home, a conversation she had forgotten all about popped into her head. And her next thought was, of course, *blackmail!* How could I have been so stupid as to miss that?

By the time she had reached her house, she knew what needed to be done but it was a bit tricky, and she could not proceed on her own. She needed Theo Oxley's help.

CHAPTER 42

On that Wednesday evening she engaged in another phone conversation with Theo. She said, "The DNA sample I submitted was not a match to the bear costume."

"I know that," Theo replied. "I talked with Lt. Sharp. But don't tell me whose DNA you submitted. I don't want to know. As I told you before, I'm interested in this case where all our book club members are concerned, but I try not to be biased."

"I have a new suspect, and this time I'm pretty sure that it is the guilty one. I will need your help to bring the person to justice, though." And she mentioned the name and told him how she had arrived at her conclusion, step by step.

He heard her out and then said, "Sounds logical, but you have no proof. How are you planning to proceed?"

"I need to obtain a DNA sample but that's difficult. I'm obviously in danger and can't ask for a meeting. I was hoping that you'd help me out. Maybe you could suggest having a drink together at The Toast?"

Theo burst out laughing with his deep throaty chuckle and said, "That would be suspicious. We've never socialized at The Toast before, and who knows, your suspect may be a teetotaler. I have a better idea. I can go for a consultation."

"A what? Ah yes, I see. That would be completely natural," she agreed. "I'd really appreciate your taking the time and effort."

"Will do. But it may take a few days, so be patient."

A bit embarrassed, she added, "And if you do obtain a sample, would you submit it directly to Lt. Sharp, please?"

"What? You don't want the credit?"

"I'm afraid that he wouldn't take me seriously if I showed up with another DNA sample."

"That's funny," he said. "I'll see to it that he takes *me* seriously."

The last thing Suzanne heard was another one of his throaty laughs, before they ended the call.

CHAPTER 43

A week later, the anticipated call from Theo came.

He said, "Mission accomplished. Between a card and a pen, there should be enough DNA to make a proper analysis."

"Thanks a million!"

Theo said, "I handed the samples to Lt. Sharp in person, but he couldn't give me an approximate date when they'd be processed. He said the lab was backlogged, and even with putting a rush on it, it would be several days."

"I have no choice but to be patient," she replied.

"There is something else I'd like to let you know. I understand why you want to solve Katherine's murder. I did some checking on my own. When you were a teenager, your younger sister accidentally drowned, and you felt responsible."

After a long pause Suzanne said, "You are correct. My kid sister was ten years younger than me and I was supposed to teach her how to swim that summer, but I never took the time. Sure, I did bring her to a local public pool a few times and did a bit of demonstrating, but she never learned properly how to swim. Our parents were on a business trip and I was in charge on the day she died. She asked me to take her swimming, but I ignored her, too busy to chat with my boyfriend on the phone. She must have decided to go for a swim on her own. The neighbors discovered her dead body in their pool over an hour later."

"I'm so sorry," he said, making his strong voice sound as gentle as possible.

"I was responsible for my sister's drowning, and since I invited Katherine into my house, I also feel responsible for what happened to her. The least I can do is avenge her murder."

Theo said, "I suspected something like that, but now I've got to run. After all, I have a regular job." And before they hung up, he added, "Promise me, no more detecting on your part at this point. It is becoming way too dangerous."

"Okay," she agreed.

Suzanne received another phone call on that day and it was from Brian. This time she did take the call.

He said, "It's good to finally hear your voice."

"Well, I don't enjoy hearing yours," she shot back. And for the next few minutes, she let loose all her built-up emotions and lashed out at him. She surprised herself by hearing the swear words coming out of her mouth, but it felt good to throw the book at him, venting some of her hurt, betrayal, and anger.

When she was done, he said, "All true. I'm so sorry. There is nothing I can say in my defense except that eight years ago, when it started, I was going through a midlife crisis."

"That is no excuse. Men go through midlife crises by taking up extreme sports, different hobbies, and affairs.

All that can maybe be forgiven, but there is no excuse or forgiveness for bigamy and for ruining two sets of families."

Brian sucked in his breath and said, "I have my punishment coming to me, I see that now. But at the end of the month I'll be stationed in L. A. again. May I come to see you and Warren?"

"No!" she stated. "You can't patch things up with me. Our rift is permanent. The only way we'll communicate in the future will be through a lawyer. As for our sons, you'll have to take it up with them. They're both old enough to make up their own minds."

Suzanne was shaking as soon as their phone conversation ended but had the satisfaction that she had stayed firm.

Brian, for his part, had tears of regret running down his cheeks, as he realized his loss to the full extent.

CHAPTER 44

The date was already Thursday, May 5, when the DNA lab result was established. To Suzanne's surprise, it was not Theo who contacted her, but Lt. Sharp. He asked for her presence at the police station. So she left the library early that day and drove over.

Again, Lt. Sharp did not get up from behind his desk but motioned her to the same chair she had sat in before. Then he came straight to the point and said, "The DNA that Theo Oxley submitted is a match with the bear costume we have in our possession as evidence."

"So I am right!" Suzanne exclaimed.

He pointed an accusing finger at her and stated, "Mrs. Morlett, you have not been straight with us from the beginning, claiming that you had no idea who your attacker was or the reason for the assault."

"When you first talked to me in the hospital, I did not know the assailant's identity, and when I brought you the first DNA sample, I had obviously suspected the wrong person." And she added, "By the way, did Theo tell you whose DNA he handed over to you?"

"No, he told me he'd leave that up to you. He did, however, mention that you and he are convinced that the attack on you is linked to an unsolved murder case. And now, Mrs. Morlett, we come to the reason I asked you here today: You need to make a statement."

"Sure."

He pressed a button and, as if on command, an officer entered his room. "This is Sgt. Tidwell. He'll record your statement."

While the sergeant got busy setting up his equipment, Lt. Sharp continued, "I want you to be aware that you're being recorded."

"No problem."

"Now then, let's proceed. Tell your story from A to Z, including the reason you were being attacked at the zoo and why you think it is linked to a murder. Most important, give us the name of the person whose DNA was submitted to us by Theo Oxley and how you came to suspect that person is the perpetrator."

So Suzanne did just that. She started at the beginning, with the book club meeting where Katherine Scherrer made her accusing remarks, to all the interviews she'd had with each club member, and in conclusion, to what she had learned from one person that led her, at long last, to pinpointing the villain.

It turned out to be a statement taking almost two hours and was exhausting. She left out her discovery about Brian's double life, determining that it was none of the police's business. Still, that fact stayed in the back of her mind, despite her effort to forget about it. Lt. Sharp was aware that making the statement took a toll on Suzanne and, at one point, he sent the sergeant to the cooler in the hallway to fetch her a cup of water.

When she had finished, the lieutenant thanked her, and the recorder was turned off. Then he stared into space for a minute before he said, "Here's the thing. I could make an arrest as far as the attack on you is concerned. We do have a DNA match, so that is clear. But as far as a murder conviction in the case of Katherine Scherrer, which so far is being treated as an accidental drowning, we have not a shred of real evidence. All we have is your gut feeling with a bit of reasoning behind it."

"So what do we do now?" Suzanne asked.

"I'm glad you said 'we.' I do have a suggestion that would involve you."

"Sure, I'm happy to help. I want this to end the correct way."

"There may be a slight risk to you, but we'll have your back."

She thought, tell me already!

"Would you consider being wired?"

"Being what? Oh, I see. I've seen enough movies to know what that is. You want me to wear a recording device."

"Precisely."

"You want me to meet with the suspect and get a confession?"

"That's the idea."

"Where?"

"I'll leave that up to you, as long as you give us enough time to wire you and have back-up units at the ready."

After the sergeant left the room, Lt. Sharp spent another few minutes preparing her by giving tips on how best to extract incriminating information from the suspect, what to do and what not to do in case of a confrontation. And Suzanne thought, aha, I'm being briefed.

From that moment onward, there was no turning back and she knew what was expected of her.

This time, Suzanne did not beat around the bush with a vague e-mail but phoned the suspect on that weekend with a request for a meeting. She said, "I know what you did and why but I'm willing to hear your side of it."

She suggested a rendezvous either at her house or the suspect's turf but both places were rejected. The culprit had anticipated this ever since the fiasco at the zoo and had had plenty of time to form a foolproof new plan to eliminate her. The scheme had been plotted and prepared down to every last detail, including a location and the purchase of a few items.

The person now suggested they meet at Montrose Park, way up high on the hill, overlooking the playground. Suzanne was familiar with the park and the proposed spot within its boundary and agreed to meet on Monday at eight o'clock in the morning.

CHAPTER 45

The stage was being set minutes before Suzanne reached the park. At 7:45, an unmarked police car pulled into the parking lot and parked. The driver killed the engine, and he and Lt. Sharp stayed in the vehicle and kept a low profile. Another unmarked car drove onto a side street next to the park's entrance, stopped against the curb, and then waited.

Five minutes later, the villain arrived on foot, checking the surroundings. There were only a few cars parked in the lot at that time in the morning. Most likely they belonged to tennis players who played a double's game at the court and some early dog walkers seen in the distance. Perfect, the culprit thought, and walked over toward the small building that housed both women and men's restrooms and then hid behind it.

At eight o'clock sharp, Suzanne pulled into the lot, parked, and left her car. She gave the park a quick glance around. She noticed a tennis game in progress and the few cars in the lot, wondering if the suspect's car was among them. Below the entrance of the park was the baseball field. She spotted a couple of people walking their dogs around the outer part of it, but the field itself was empty. She passed the playground with its swings, slides, and other equipment, which was also deserted that Monday morning. Then she slowly made her way up the steep hill to the rendezvous place.

Once Suzanne had passed the restrooms, the culprit came out of hiding and walked over to where her car was parked. The person reached into a small paper bag, removed a device, and attached it nonchalantly to the bottom of her vehicle near the exhaust pipe. Then the person tossed the empty bag into the nearest trash bin and also hiked up the hill.

"Did you see that?" Lt. Sharp in the unmarked car asked.

"Sure did," the driver replied.

"I doubt that it's on a timer; the suspect would not have a clue what to set it to."

"Must be programmed to go off remotely by phone."

"Yep!"

"I'll keep an eye on it."

"Quiet, their interview is about to begin," said the lieutenant.

CHAPTER 46

Suzanne sat at the upper most bench and table at the park and saw him climbing up the hill toward her at a fast pace. At first, she did not recognize him, dressed in a business suit and dress shoes, with a baseball cap covering his bald head. Under different circumstances, his getup would have been comical.

Slightly out of breath, he plopped himself onto the bench across from her and said, "So tell me what you know, or think that you know."

"A good morning to you too, Luke!" she announced, hoping the police officers would be tuned in.

"I'm not in the mood for pleasantries, so start talking. This had better not be another bluff of yours, like you've pulled all along."

Suzanne agreed, "It's true that in the past I made a few shots in the dark, but that was then. Now I have facts to back it up."

"Like what?"

"Your current record and reputation as financial advisor is clean and beyond reproach, but your slate wasn't all that spotless in the past when you worked as accountant to a major tech company. There was an investigation of embezzlement. Now, isn't that the truth?"

"It was dropped for lack of enough evidence. I made sure to cover my tracks," he replied. And his arrogance was even more apparent as he added, "The statute of limitations has long run out, even if new evidence came to light."

She let her sunglasses slide down to the tip of her nose and, looking him in the eye, said, "But your reputation and consequently the livelihood of your current immaculate business would be at stake if word got around that you were a crook. Right? I mean, who would trust you with investing their hard-earned money, knowing that you might misappropriate it?"

Luke did not answer but stared at her with menace.

She continued, "I knew all along that blackmail was the key to solving the mystery of Katherine's death. I figured out that even though she had no intention to blackmail anyone, her killer believed that blackmail was exactly what she was after. For a long time, I couldn't pinpoint who among our book club members that could be, but recently, I recalled a conversation I'd had with your ex-wife and…"

He interrupted, "You talked with Narissa? Why the heck did you do that, and how did you even find her?"

"A real estate agent by the name of Narissa Grey was not hard to locate; you told me her first name yourself on the occasion of our interview. But never mind that. As I was saying, during my chat with Narissa, she let something slip. I mentioned that you were less than happy to have to pay alimony, and she was amused and remarked, 'That's what Luke calls it? I prefer to think of it as hush money.'"

He sucked in his breath as Suzanne went on, "At the time that remark went over my head, but not too long ago,

I remembered her comment and what it meant. Narissa has been blackmailing you for years, and you jumped to the conclusion that Katherine Scherrer was about to do the same."

Now the angry words dashed out of his mouth like a torrent. "The bitch! I've been her goldmine for more than a decade and it's never going to end. In my bookkeeping I post the monthly expense as alimony, but it's blackmail money, sure as hell. She knows that she can ruin me by spreading gossip about my past. I can't ever silence her; as her ex I'd be the prime suspect. And yes, the damn author was about to do the same. I could ill afford to pay two blackmailers for the rest of my life."

"So you had to silence Katherine?"

There was a rustling of leaves coming from the shrubs nearby. Spooked, he jerked his head to one side and asked, "What was that?"

"Most likely just a rabbit or maybe a lizard. I doubt there are snakes up here." And without missing a beat she said, "You didn't answer my question."

"What question?"

"That you had to silence Katherine."

"I had no choice. But there is no evidence that I did," was his cocky answer.

"You're wrong there. Your phone call to Katherine can be traced."

"So I called her and had a chat. That's not against the law."

Suzanne probed, "Let's get to the attack on me at the zoo, then. That was to stop me from investigating Katherine's murder."

He shot back, "You can't prove that the attacker was me. In fact, you have no idea who was under that bear costume."

"Surely your DNA is all over that costume you wore."

"Maybe, but the cops didn't obtain any DNA from me to match it with, now, did they?" It was a rhetorical question and he continued, "And don't think you can sneak it off me now. I'm watching you like a hawk."

Suzanne caught herself before saying something that she should not. Lt. Sharp had instructed her not to mention that the police were in possession of his DNA and that it was a match.

Instead she said, "Speaking of the bear character. I'm curious, how did you manage to put the person who originally wore the bear costume out of commission?"

Luke could not resist bragging about how clever he was and said, "That was child's play. You mix chlorine bleach with isopropyl alcohol, and voila, you've got chloroform, which puts a person out like a light when held under his nose."

A young man in athletic shorts came jogging up the hill, circled around to where the two were sitting, and then ran down the slope again. This seemed to spook Luke once more, and Suzanne realized that his so-called confession had come to an end.

As soon as the jogger was out of sight, Luke got up and said, "Enough! We're done." His voice turned to steel as he ordered, "You're going to follow my instructions to the letter, understood?" And as she nodded and got up likewise, he reached under his suit jacket and pulled out a gun.

CHAPTER 47

Lt. Sharp said, "Show and tell is over; they're walking down the hill," and he alerted the officers in the unmarked car parked at the next street and also some of the regular force on standby. Then he and his subordinate got out of the car and watched Suzanne and Luke's approach from up the hill.

"Hard to tell from that distance, but it looks like he's got a weapon on her," he remarked.

"Yes, sir."

Lt. Sharp motioned to the other officer and they took cover behind the restroom building.

Suzanne listened to Luke's orders while he marched her down the incline, aware of the gun pressing against her back.

He said, "You won't get hurt if you do exactly what I'm instructing you to do. I knew this day would come and planned accordingly. Timing is of the utmost importance. I'm going to walk you down to your car and you'll drive up Angeles Crest Highway, all the way to the Switzer picnic area."

Suzanne felt the pressure on her back increase as he continued, "I placed explosives under your car, which I'll control remotely with my phone. I know that you'll contact the police, if you haven't done so already. I'm going to make a deal with them. Your life for my freedom."

"What do you mean?" she stammered.

"I came prepared. I have a flight reservation to a country with no extradition. I'll call 911 from the airport and make my proposal and demand."

They were almost at the playground as Suzanne said, "I still don't get it."

"It will take about the same amount of time for you to drive to the Switzer Camp in the Angeles Forest as it'll take me to get to the airport. The police will take the deal; they can't afford not to. Now, I want you to know that I can track you and will be aware of your driving progress. If you drive anywhere else but the 210 freeway and up Angeles Crest, I'll know and won't hesitate to blow your car to pieces. Understood?"

All she could muster was a nod.

They arrived at her car and she asked, "Where did you park?"

"I live around the corner and came on foot. No more chit chat. Get in the car."

She unlocked it and, with the gun still aimed on her, he motioned her into the driver seat. He then held out his other hand and ordered, "Hand me your phone."

"Please let me keep it, I won't call anyone," she begged.

He stamped his foot and yelled, "Hand it over pronto!"

She rummaged in her purse and then gave it to him.

Before shutting her door, he said, "Now drive straight to the Switzer Camp and no detour, or you won't know what hit you!"

As she drove out of the parking lot, Luke walked over to the same trash bin where he had earlier discarded an empty bag and tossed the gun.

Suzanne was on a surface street a couple of blocks away from the park and was headed toward the East 210 Freeway. She kept thinking, it's crazy and makes no sense at all. Why is he sending me up Angeles Crest? If he would be next to me, holding the gun to my face and making me drive up to the woods where there'd be no witnesses if he'd shot me, I could see the point. But this thing about blowing the car up if I drove somewhere else is total rubbish. On the other hand, if it is true that he attached explosives to the car and that he is tracking me, if I don't do as I'm told, he may pull that remote trigger he warned me of.

At that point in her thought process she heard a slew of sirens, which seemed to come from the park she had left seconds ago. At the same time there was a police car behind her, waving her over to stop.

Do I dare risk it? she asked herself. What if Luke's tracking device shows that I stop? Oh, what the heck! For all he knows I could be stopped at a traffic light. With a sudden jerk she stepped on the brake and came to a halt at the curb.

She left the motor running, just in case. She rolled down her window as the officer stepped up to her car.

"Hello, ma'am. Lt. Sharp sent me. He said you're no longer in danger, and the guilty person is being arrested."

"Boy, am I glad to hear that," she said, while suddenly shedding tears of relief.

Then she pulled herself together and said, "There may be explosives attached to my car. Is it safe for me to drive home?"

"We deactivated the device, but we need to tow your vehicle in for evidence. I'll give you a ride to the station where you'll get de-wired and we can make arrangement for a rental car.

CHAPTER 48

Three days later, at the end of her workday, Suzanne sat in Lt. Sharp's office once more. She had collected her car early that morning, but it was not until six in the evening that they both made time for a meeting.

He started by thanking her for her part in bringing a murderer to justice, and then complimenting her with, "You sure hold up well under pressure."

"Thanks, but I wasn't as confident as I tried to sound. Actually, the entire encounter with Luke felt like being in a bad dream, especially when he walked me down the hill."

"Oh, before I forget," said the lieutenant, "I believe this belongs to you." And he handed her cellphone over.

"Thanks! I felt lost without it."

"And now I'm sure you have some questions concerning Luke Grey. Since you were a big help in apprehending him, I feel you have a certain right to the facts."

Suzanne said, "I know that you placed him under arrest. The officer who caught up with me before I got to the 210 Freeway told me so. But did he confess?"

"He sure did. When we informed him that the entire conversation between him and you had been recorded, and we even played portions of it back to him, he confessed everything."

"There is tons of stuff puzzling me. Could he really have activated the device via his phone?"

"Affirmative. We saw him attach the device and switched it off, but his phone could have activated it."

"What about the tracking gadget he bragged about?"

"That was pure fabrication; there was none," said the detective.

"And the plan about calling 911 from the airport and making a deal - - sparing me my life for his freedom - - before catching a flight to some obscure place?"

"All fiction! The man has an overstimulated imagination. He wasn't going to any airport and he didn't have tickets to fly to some remote destination. He needed a somewhat plausible explanation for sending you up to the Switzer Camp on your own."

Suzanne sucked in her breath and said, "I'm beginning to understand why he sent me up there. At the time I thought that he wanted me to have no contact with any human being until he himself got to the airport. Now I get it. He wanted me up in the forest away from people, where I had no access to human contact, period."

Lt. Sharp looked at her with something like fatherly concern and stated, "If you'd have made it up to the camp, and maybe even sooner, he'd have activated the explosives, as soon as he had established his alibi. But that wasn't going to happen on my watch."

She stared at him, uncomprehending.

He explained, "He had planned to walk the short distance to his house, hop in his car, and drive to his business location in Pasadena, where he had an appointment scheduled with a client."

"Now it makes sense that he was wearing a suit. I thought his getup was strange for a meeting in the park."

Suzanne let it all sink in for a moment, then suddenly exclaimed, "My God! He would have activated the bomb under my car once he got to his office and I'd have been stranded in it, like a sitting duck."

After a pause, she asked, "But why come to the park on foot? I mean, having his car there would have been more efficient."

"That was rather clever of him," said the lieutenant. "He wanted no trace of him being anywhere near Montrose Park." And he added, "The man is clever in many ways, but not checking you for wires was a huge mistake. I was counting on that, since he's an amateur and not a professional criminal."

She wanted to know, "What if he had checked me for a recording device?"

With a smile, he assured her, "In that case, you would have been in immediate danger and we'd have stepped in and taken over."

"What's happening now? Is he going to prison for the rest of his life?"

"I can't answer that. It's out of our hands. Even if a person makes a confession, he or she still has the right to a jury trial. In Luke Grey's case, the facts speak for themselves, but one never knows what a good defense lawyer will come up with. And as far as the sentencing goes, the fact that he did not threaten you in the park with an actual weapon may impress the jury in his favor and sway them to some leniency."

She protested, "But he *did* threaten me with a weapon. I saw the gun and felt it on my back when he forced me to walk down the hill and get into my car."

"That was a toy gun. We saw him tossing it into a trash bin at the park and collected it. He counted on the fact that you wouldn't know the difference, and he was right."

Suzanne was a bit embarrassed about that, but he didn't seem to notice.

"Speaking of the trial, in my estimation, it will be several months from now, but you will need to testify."

"Oh, I didn't think that far ahead. I guess I won't have a choice in the matter and will do my duty," she said.

The meeting was over. Lt. Sharp thanked her again, and she got up to leave. She was already at the door when he said, "Let me know if you'd be willing to do undercover assignments for us in the future."

She turned and stared, unsure whether or not he was serious. Then she noticed the twitch at the corner of his mouth and the mischief in his eyes and answered, "That depends on what you're willing to pay!"

CHAPTER 49

Early one morning in July, before it got too hot, Suzanne went for a stroll at Crescenta Valley Park. She took a break at the skateboard court and got comfortable on the bleachers.

The court was empty, except for a man and his five-year-old boy. The little kid had on a helmet and wore knee and elbow pads for protection, making him look like a miniature mummy. The boy was getting a lesson in skateboarding, and Suzanne watched as his dad patiently guided him down a steep grade in the arena, trying to get enough speed to rise up the incline on the opposite side.

This went on without success for numerous tries. He either slid back at the crucial moment or fell off the board. She marveled at the little guy's stamina. As she thought to herself, 'give it a rest, tomorrow is another day,' the boy and his skateboard made it up the mount in one piece. She couldn't help herself but clapped and yelled "Bravo!"

At 7:30 a.m., Theo Oxley came jogging along. He was about to pass by the bleachers and did a double take when he spotted Suzanne.

He stopped his run, plopped himself next to her, waited for his breathing to get back to normal, and then asked, "Are you stalking me?"

She returned his banter and admitted, "That's one way of putting it. I hoped to find you here." And she continued, "Lt. Sharp must have kept you in the loop about Luke's arrest and his awaiting trial for murder."

Theo nodded. "He told me all about your part in bringing him to justice. I'm impressed. Playing your role took guts."

"I wasn't fishing for compliments," she said. "In fact, I want to put the entire experience behind me, but I'm curious about something."

Theo watched the little boy on the court getting better and more daring on his skateboard and remarked, "I guess one has to start early in life to become a champ." Then he turned back to Suzanne and asked, "What do you want to know?"

"You never told me how you went about getting a DNA sample from Luke. I remember you mentioning something about a card and a pen, but you didn't go into details."

"It was easier than I had anticipated. I called his office and asked to make an appointment for a consultation in the late afternoon or early evening. When I got there, his secretary was about to leave for the day but offered me a beverage, which I declined. I told Luke a poppycock story about a substantial inheritance from my aunt I was in the process of receiving, asking for investment advice.

"He was happy to run the numbers for me on the computer, displaying them on his large monitor. There were annuities, stocks, bonds, hedge funds, and all sorts of investments I had never heard of, which he tried to explain to me. He calculated the percentage of return for each, and the pros and cons for a long- or short-term investment. He also pointed out the risks involved for moderate versus conservative securities."

Theo smiled and said, "I didn't pretend to understand any of it. He gave me a prospectus and his business card, which I did not touch and left at the edge of his desk. At some point during his presentation, I told him that I'd changed my mind and would like some coffee. He went to get it in the next room. During his short absence, I shoved the card into a small plastic baggie I had at the ready, without touching it, using the prospectus to guide it along. And just in case there wasn't enough of his DNA on the business card, I filched a pen he had lying on the desk and also slid that into the baggie without touching it."

He laughed and said, "The hardest part for me was to stay put after that, having to listen to his spiel for another half hour, until he finally wrapped it up. He handed over some more brochures from different investment companies and said I should think it over and then we would go from there."

"Now it's my turn to be impressed," Suzanne stated.

"I had better continue my run before I get too lazy. Come by for a chat again; you'll find me here every morning." He waved to her and was gone.

Suzanne stayed seated on the bleachers for a long while after he had jogged on, and even after the father and his little boy had left the skateboard court. She played the events of the last few months back in her mind. Once again they did not seem real to her, feeling more like a disturbing movie. Then she looked at her empty ring finger and wondered if she would ever be able to get over it all.

EPILOGUE

A jury convicted Luke Grey of premeditated murder in the case of Katherine Scherrer and attempted murder of Suzanne Morlett. The sentencing took place a few days later. Since the criminal showed remorse, he received 50 years in prison, rather than life without the possibility of parole. Considering Luke's age of 47, the man would be nearly 100 by the time he'd be released. Chances were slim that he would ever regain his freedom.

Suzanne had to testify at the trial, which brought the entire horrific experience back into the foreground of her mind.

There were mixed feelings among Katherine's family. Some felt gratified that justice had been served, but others would have preferred to keep thinking of her passing as an accident.

Because of the game the author played with the book club members for her amusement, and Luke's reaction to it, several people's lives - - in addition to the ones of her family - - were forever changed.

The murderer's ex-wife, Narissa Grey, lost her goldmine, but was lucky not to be tried and convicted of blackmail. The pay-offs had been posted as alimony on Luke's books, so there was no proof of her crime.

For the Morletts a divorce was inevitable. Their rift was too deep for any chance of repair. Suzanne could never forgive Brian his double life, and he in return was unable to get over the fact that she had thought him capable of murder.

Lillian could not bring herself to tell Ali the truth about her father. How does one explain bigamy to a seven-year-old? For now, the story she told her child was that Daddy no longer had assignments to fly the East Coast route. She planned to enlighten Ali of the sordid facts sometime in the distant future.

Finally, the book club. It fell apart. For its members, there were too many reminders of dark secrets kept - - and how they suspected each other of committing murder - - to be simply forgotten and buried.

After all, Theo Oxley hit the nail on the head when he called it a "dark" book club.

Stand-Alone Mysteries by Alice Zogg

A Dark Book Club

A Bad Apple

Exposing the Past

No Curtain Call

The Ill-Fated Scientist

Accidental Eyewitness

A Bet Turned Deadly

R. A. Huber Mysteries by Alice Zogg

Evil at Shore Haven

Guilty or Not
Murder at the Cubbyhole

Revamp Camp

Final Stop Albuquerque

The Fall of Optimum House

The Lonesome Autocrat

Tracking Backward

Turn the Joker Around

Reaching Checkmate